A profile of the author

Susan Westoby is an ex teacher in her early 40s living in a home in Roby Liverpool which she, her husband, and her father built for themselves.

She was born and lived most of her childhhod in Knotty Ash and, after passing the eleven-plus attended Childwall Valley High School.

Her teacher condemed her for being too creative and not analytical enough in her writing, so, whilst in the lower 6th she left and spent the next 2 years in Millbank College of Commerce.

Her passionate interest in books attracted her to work in the Liverpool City Libraries but after 2 years she decided to turn to teaching: She enrolled and completed a 3 year course at C. S. Mott College in Prescot studying Mediaeval history; the results of which which she has put to good use in this, her first novel.

The Westoby household has 2 foster children and an assortment of animals i.e. 7 dogs, 7 horses and ponies, chickens and hens, cats of colours and hues, an Oriental pig, and various other animals and fowl — a very lively bunch indeed.

Susan is at the present moment writing a further book entitled **Brave Heart** which is planned for early next Spring.

Judging by **Saxon Falcon** her first novel Susan has undoubtedly, a wealth of talent just waiting to be unleashed — *we have not heard the last of her by any means.*

The publisher

Dedication

My grateful thanks to Carol and Debbie for
their continual encouragement and support
during the writing of this book.

ISBN 0 903348 47 0

Cover design by Arthur Diamond Liverpool

Typeset in Palatino by
Print Origination Formby, Liverpool L37 8EG
Printed and bound in Great Britain by
The Cromwell Press, Melksham, Wiltshire

Saxon Falcon

Saxon Falcon

by

Susan E. Westoby

Print Origination
Formby Merseyside L37 8EG

Contents

1

They had spent the whole of August chafing at the contrary winds which kept them in Normandy. After months of preparation for the invasion of England, William, Duke of Normandy, and his carefully gathered forces, were forced to kick their heels and wait; wait for the wind to change direction; to sweep the cockle-shell boats, painstakingly built, begged and stolen, across the narrow sea to where Harold Godwineson steadily watched the Channel for an attack.

In September a westerly gale struck and the ships were forced from the Estuary of the River Dives, up the coast to Saint Valery, in the territory of Guy, Count of Ponthieu. In the gale, ships were lost, and their crews buried in haste. Some troops deserted and only a brilliant commander such as William could have rallied his bored and discouraged army.

"Even here the wind is wrong."

Michel du Fourmeils, Lord of Tierand and Quatre Bras, watched with jaundiced eye the religious procession as it wound its way through the town. The body of Saint Valery had been taken from the church in a desperate attempt to enlist God's aid and the soldiers sent up fervent prayers for a favourable breeze.

"There is a change in the air. I can smell it."

Ralf de Regny sniffed optimistically and cocked an eyebrow

at the sky. "This will be our last night on shore. Best make the most of it."

The Lord du Fourmeils grinned at his friend.

"'Tis your Viking blood my friend. I admit you are rarely wrong. Come then, let us seek a warm tavern with friendly wenches to bid us Godspeed."

The following morning, September 27th, Ralf de Regny's prediction was proved correct. The wind backed south, and in the evening William embarked his troops.

The Norman forces took to those fragile boats with glee, and a high enthusiasm, which lasted only as long as it took for their stomachs to reject all that they had eaten or drunk in the last few hours.

The Lord du Fourmeils leaned retching over the rail of the shallow transport and wondered why he had ever agreed to join William in his claim for the crown of England. He had no need of land. As well as his holding in Normandy, Quatre Bras, which he had inherited from his father, Michel already had lands in England. The manor of Tierand was his from his mother's father in the absence of other male heirs.

A grunt and a groan from his side signalled the arrival of Ralf de Regny and Michel essayed a twisted grin at his old and trusted friend. Ralf had stood by him and often guided him through many a campaign in William the Bastard's fight to secure his duchy. That had been in the early days when there were many who sought to wrest William's birthright from him.

"God, I hope this is worth it. I hope William remembers our fidelity and our fortitude in this venture."

Michel grimaced as his stomach protested once more against the heavy swell of the Channel.

"Fear not my friend. The Duke will amply reward all those who follow him so stoutly in this crusade."

The Norman lord did not use the phrase lightly. William had spent much energy in persuading the Pope to support his claim to the English throne. The price was not high. Simply to remove Archbishop Stigand from the see of Canterbury.

Stigand had been condemned by successive Popes for holding the Archbishopric while his predecessor still lived. The word 'crusade' had taken William's fancy and now he delighted in its use at every opportunity.

Ralf de Regny closed his eyes and wiped the spittle from his chin. He was no longer a young man. He was in this to gain lands, for himself and his heirs. Heirs! He smiled grimly. He did not even have a wife. Not any longer. Marie de Regny had died of the bloody flux almost ten years ago. The child had died with her!

He sighed and shrugged. Perhaps William would provide a new wife also.

Anything was possible.

The Norman fleet had made an unmolested night crossing and it was a fine morning when the army disembarked on the Sussex coast near Pevensey. The disadvantages of the town of Pevensey as a base were immediately obvious. Surrounded by salt marshes and interlaced with innumerable channels, the place was a deathtrap.

Watching the carpenters hastily assemble the ready built sections of fortifications, Ralf de Regny shivered and huddled into his cloak, squinting around to discover Michel carefully checking over his warhorse as the squire struggled to hold it. The animal was obviously delighted to find itself once more on firm land as it danced and sidled and Ralf thanked God that his own stallion had survived the trip also free from injury. The beasts were expensive enough without the added hazards of a sea-borne journey to deal with.

They spent that night in relative comfort and security before setting out towards what was by all accounts the more easily defensible harbour of Hastings. There the Norman forces dug in and waited. Waited for Harold Godwineson to come south.

Michel du Fourmeils and Ralf de Regny carefully checked and rechecked their equipment, their stores, the well-being of their forces. Each lord had a sizeable following; Michel's made up mainly from men from his Norman lands at Quatre Bras, with an additional complement of mercenaries, men, however, who had fought with him before, and whom he could trust.

In the comfort of the quarters they shared, Ralf watched and grinned as his friend stripped and washed, stretching the stiffness from his lean, muscular frame. The lad was never short of female admirers, yet he had never yet set his heart on one fair face. He would have to decide soon. There were no heirs to the lands he held but a distant cousin, and that cousin's tastes were such as to make him an undesirable lord for Tierand and Quatre Bras.

Saer de Friese was a cousin of Michel's mother and his sexual preferences were for men or young boys. Ralf grimaced to himself in distaste. If Saer had not been the cruel and evil beast he was, then his leanings would not have mattered a jot to Ralf or Michel. As it was, he was deeply depraved, and if Ralf had been in Michel's place, a well aimed dagger would have put paid to Saer and his ambitions for good.

* * *

William was king sooner than anyone could have reasonably expected.

On 14th October the Norman army, marching north from Hastings, came on the English on the edge of the great forest known as the Weald.

William's strokes of fortune continued. Harold had come south with great speed after defeating the Viking Harald Hardrada at Stamford Bridge. He had only a small army with him. He did not wait for reinforcements but engaged William immediately.

For hours the English front stood firm. Then the Normans, retreating from an attack, fell into confusion, and some of the English broke ranks to attack them. The Normans rallied and cut down their pursuers; then attacked, and twice feigned a confused retreat, on both occasions drawing the English to follow them. By now the English front was seriously weakened, and soon after, in another major attack, Harold himself was killed.

William marched slowly on London, sweeping through Sussex, Surrey and Hertfordshire in a great figure of eight. He laid the countryside waste as he went, leaving no-one in any doubt what it meant to cross him.

After a few weeks, the English leaders submitted; and on Christmas Day 1066 he was annointed and crowned in Westminster Abbey.

* * *

Michel du Fourmeils and Ralf de Regny stood in front of their king and eyed him warily as he pored over some maps on the great table before him. A sufficient number of English earls and thegns had fallen at Hastings to provide the king with land to reward the most outstanding or grasping of his followers.

Michel had his grandfather's holding at Tierand, but although it had come to him legally through his mother who had been a Saxon, it was vital that William should confirm Michel's title to the lands, and accept his oath of fealty.

Ralf, however, needed a grant of some Saxon holding. As a third son he had always been landless and footloose, depending on hiring out his services to various warring lords, more lately William, to make a living.

The king finally looked up and crooked his finger at the two men before him. As they moved forward he surveyed them thoughtfully before directing their attention to the map spread out for his perusal.

"Thus far we have succeeded, and succeeded well. The matter, however, lies not with the taking so much as with the keeping."

The two men listening nodded their understanding, not only of his words but of the reasoning behind them. William knew by bitter experience that a successful ruler had to be feared, and he reckoned this was even more true of a successful usurper. In the grant of lands already bestowed all had contained the proviso that a castle be built at the lord's own expense, particularly at key places and in many of the larger towns. Michel and Ralf waited expectantly.

The king's finger moved along the map, north from London until it stabbed at a point some few days' ride away.

"Sensgarth manor. Its master, the lord Rufus. The sons killed at Senlac, the daughters...marriageable?"

William paused a moment, enjoying the uncertainty of the lords before him.

"I wish to ensure the loyalty of Lord Rufus and to be certain that this manor will not be used against me in any possible uprisings. I wish this to be done as peacefully as possible. The most obvious way is to marry the daughters to certain worthy lords on whom I can rely. You understand I trust?"

Michel and Ralf simply nodded.

"You, my Lord du Fourmeils, lay claim to your grandfather's holding, through your mother...Tierand?"

"Yes Sire."

"Well then your claim will be stronger if you have a wife and possibility of heirs to inherit. A Saxon wife would be— diplomatic, I feel."

"Yes Sire."

Lord Ralf almost held his breath as the king moved his finger once more over the map, coming back towards the south but moving a little eastwards.

"Runesay! Without a lord through no fault of ours. A suitable reward for one who has long fought for me most hardily. What say you my Lord de Regny?"

"I am most grateful Sire."

"Be sure that is what I expect. You also need a wife. I believe there are several daughters at Sensgarth." The king raised his head and narrowed his eyes.

"I trust to your diplomacy my lords. Be sure you take a sufficient force to deter resentment. Good hunting. I shall expect you here again as soon as your tasks are done. And now, if you will excuse me?"

Michel and Ralf bowed their heads and left the room.

Neither man spoke until they were on the road out of the city to where their forces were encamped, then Ralf was the first to speak.

"The king is most generous — lands *and* a wife."

Michel laughed shortly.

"Tis true we all need a wife, if only to breed heirs. I only pray God they are young and clean and sound in wind and limb. I would have preferred to choose for myself."

"You sound as though you are choosing a horse."

"That would be easier than this in my reckoning."

At dawn the next day the two lords set out to the north. The countryside seemed empty and forlorn and the men huddled deep into their cloaks as protection against the cold wind.

It was William's intention to maintain a continuity of rule in order to give as much feasibility as possible to his claim to the English throne. The Saxons for the moment were quiet. Those who had survived the battle of invasion and William's subsequent progress to London and his coronation, had crept homewards. To lick their wounds and regain their strength. For what? To serve William as their now acknowledged king? Or to turn against him in rebellion? William did not intend that they should have the chance to decide.

Michel and Ralf were faced with a dilemma. They needed to secure Runesay for Ralf but also they needed to reach Sensgarth as quickly as possible. Michel beckoned to one of his men.

"Gerd. Take a detachment of your men and make haste to Tierand. Secure the gates and wait for me."

The man bent his head, "Yes Lord," and moved away quickly snapping out orders to about twenty of the warriors in the company.

"It is Runesay we need to worry about."

Ralf frowned.

"Sir Roger will handle that I think. We don't know what he may find but I can trust him."

"He will need enough men with him in case of trouble, but we cannot spare too many ourselves."

Michel glanced over their force.

"He will need at least fifty men."

Sir Roger, and Ralf and Michel's other knights were watch-

ing them expectantly. It took only a few minutes to give them
their orders before Sir Roger took his leave with a pleased expression on his face. The rest of the Norman force resumed its
steady but purposeful march on Sensgarth. It took them three
days.

"We should reach Sensgarth towards evening."

They had not made camp. Simply dismounted and rested
their horses. loosening the girths and giving ther animals
water and some grain.

Ralf munched on some hard dry bread.

"They probably know we're here. They'll be expecting us."

Michel nodded.

"Let's hope the Lord of Sensgarth is a sensible man. They
could not hope to win a confrontation with us. You do the talk-
ing, Ralf, if we get that far. This has to be done well. William
expects a lot from us and I, for one, dare not fail."

The spectre of Saer de Friese loomed. Michel knew that his
cousin would delight in his failure. He would be waiting to
snatch at Michel's lands at the first opportunity.

The gates of Sensgarth were closed, sentries manned the
walls. The holding was in a good position. The forest had been
cleared well back and the hall and stockade were built on a
small rise. Slightly larger than the other Saxon halls which
Michel had known, the defences were good.

They sat and waited for the challenge, and when it came
Michel answered in the Saxon tongue, thanking heaven for his
Saxon grandfather.

"The Lords du Fourmeils and de Regny on King William's
business with the Lord of Sensgarth. We are on a peaceful task
here and not intent on harm."

There was a surprised pause after he spoke then slowly the
great gates opened and Michel glanced at Ralf before kneeing
his horse forward.

They could feel the tension as they rode through into the
courtyard. Hard eyes watched them as they dismounted, and
although the guards had no arrows knocked to the strings,
nevertheless their bows were in their hands.

They left their main force outside the gates and only their knights and about twenty of their men went into the stronghold with them.

The Lord of Stensgarth stood at the door of his hall, strong and proud.

"If you will follow me my lords."

Lord Rufus of Stensgarth turned heavily and preceded the Normans into the hall. He mounted the dais at the far end and turned to face them before sitting in his great chair.

"Now state your business."

Ralf drew forth the documents which William had given them, and which laid out the terms under which Lord Rufus had the chance to keep his lands and his position.

Lord Rufus read through them slowly and laboriously, breaking the silence now and then with a question.

Finally he leaned back and glared defiantly at them. Michel and Ralf tensed simultaneously.

The torch flames flickered in their brackets, casting a weird leaping light on the scene in the great hall at Sensgarth.

Edith watched mesmerised, from her hiding place in the bend of the stairs as her father glared defiantly at the Norman lords standing before him.

The armed warriors ringing the hall behind them sharpened Lord Rufus's sense of helplessness yet they could not quell the courage and pride evident in his broad squat figure. These men had come to ensure his obedience to William's laws, but he refused to cower before them.

Lord Rufus's holding was small but rich, and occupied a key point on the road to the north. William had sent his most trusted men to take it; peacefully if possible, but adequately supported if not.

Edith studied the warrior facing her father. He was tall and heavily built. Clean shaven as were all the Normans, he had pushed back his mailed hood to reveal short cropped dark hair, sprinkled with grey like hoar frost on a boar's bristles. His similarity to the animal did not end there. His eyes were small and close set, glinting with anger as he gestured to the armed men at his back.

"You are in no position to defy William as you can see," he rumbled. "The terms are very generous if you are sensible. If not..." he shrugged his shoulders and gave a short laugh.

Lord Rufus's body slumped in defeat as he reached out once more to the documents which had been placed before him, scanning them grimly, then casting them away from him as he spoke.

"Very well, it seems I have no choice."

Although her father's voice and gesture were weary and there were no Saxon warriors to support him should he roar defiance, Edith sensed the relief which whispered through the Norman ranks. These men were tired and cold after the long march north. William had given his army no respite in the bid to secure England and the troops crowding the hall stretched muscles cramped from the northern wind. Their eyes brightened with anticipation as Lord Rufus's servants hurried to set up tables and benches to accommodate them in Sensgarth hall.

Panic reigned in the kitchens as the cooks laboured to provide food for so many and to complete the tasks left standing when the Norman force had approached. And what if a long-bladed knife or deadly meat hook were skilfully and perhaps a little regretfully concealed? What if they were returned to a less deadly purpose than had been intended when they were snatched up? Lord Rufus's people were no cowards.

As the bustle started in the hall below her, Edith turned and hurried back up the stairs to the chamber she shared with her two sisters. She carried in her mind the image of her mother, the Lady Beatrice, placing a comforting hand over that of her lord before he indicated to the Normans that they should take their place at his table. Lord Rufus held fast to his wife's fingers as she rose to be introduced to the men who were to enforce William's peace terms on this holding, and to be informed of the part her daughters were to play in those terms.

In blissful ignorance of the effect William's peace settlement was to have on her life and on the lives of her sisters, Edith pushed aside the curtains over the entrance to their room and stopped as she met the questioning grey gaze of Mathild, her older sister. Mathild and Edwina had not ventured forth as had Edith to take a closer look at William's men, and although Mathild was outwardly calm her inner agitation was revealed by the twisting of her long, graceful fingers in her amber necklace, a gift from her betrothed before his departure to fight for Harold at Stamford Bridge. He, like so many others, had never returned.

Edith wondered what was going on in the mind behind those clear grey eyes but was swiftly distracted by Edwina's weeping. She knelt and placed a comforting arm about her younger sister's shoulders. Edwina was but twelve years of age and Edith wondered how William's terms would affect her. Surely she was too young to become a pawn in the Norman's political game. Edith prayed that this was so.

The heavy curtain at the door rustled as their mother entered. She stopped a moment and took a breath, avoiding their eyes as she spoke.

"You are summoned to eat with our guests," a faint inflexion on the last word, "You must hurry and change."

She knelt with a flurry of skirts at the large chest where the girls kept their best outfits, and raising the lid started to pull out the garments. Her hands shook and as Mathild stooped to help her, the Lady Beatrice turned and in a strange reversal of roles the daughter crooned and rocked the heaving body of her mother in her arms.

"My doves, my doves," sobbed Lady Beatrice, "What will these crude Norman pigs do with my precious doves."

"Hush mother, do not carry on so, one man is much like another. His desires are the same wherever he is born." Mathild's voice held a hint of scorn which surprised and faintly shocked Edith and silenced Lady Beatrice enough for Edith to step into the pause.

"I shall wear my new yellow gunna and the gold bliaut. We must show these foreign lords that we are no peasants to be treated with contempt, but ladies of the same good Saxon blood that they spilled on Senlac field."

With an effort Lady Beatrice controlled herself and steeled

her heart to tell her daughters of William's intent to marry that good Saxon blood to his Norman lords.

"My dears, you must prepare yourselves...," her voice faltered then she raised her chin and held them with her glance. "It is the Norman's intentions to take themselves Saxon wives. You are to be presented to your future lords as soon as you are ready and the marriages will take place with all speed."

The unbelieving silence lengthened until Lady Beatrice could bear to look on their stricken faces no longer and turned away to busy herself once more with the clothes in the chest. Edith forced herself to move to her mother's side, and disguising the sense of shock which held her attempted a matter of fact tone.

"Well, at least we are to be wed and not raped indiscriminately."

Edwina gasped but Mathild gave a short, bitter laugh.

"What difference a ring on our finger if we still bed with a hog."

Edith looked consideringly at her sister, the image of the tall Norman facing her father in her mind, then making a determined effort they started to prepare themselves for what they all felt was to be an ordeal in the hall below.

Edith's mind seethed with speculation as they descended the stairs. Her stomach was gripped by a tight knot and the palms of her hands were sticky with sweat. Forcing herself to relax her tightly balled fists she rubbed her hands down the skirt of the yellow gunna and took a breath to calm herself. Of all Lord Rufus's children Edith had been the one most ignored by her father. Never an indulgent parent, he never even seemed to realise that Edith existed. This attitude seemed to rub off on the other inhabitants of the holding, and perhaps it was because of this that Edith at seventeen was still unbetrothed. This fact had never really bothered Edith. Her heart had never quickened at a male glance and those friends of her brothers' who had visited the holding had scarcely glanced at the middle sister with the soft brown eyes and demure brown braids.

All eyes had been for Mathild whose cool blonde looks and

graceful figure had attracted many languishing sighs from young lords.

Edith slid a surreptitious glance towards Mathild. Her sister was too calm. Although never one to show her emotions, Edith had expected more reaction from her, especially as her fondness for Edward, her betrothed, had seemed so deep. Her grief at the news of his death had left her eyes swollen for many days afterwards.

A small damp hand slid into Edith's and she gave a start then squeezed the hand gently. Edwina had also inherited more than a fair share of her father's blonde attractiveness. Surely she would not be forced into marriage yet? A betrothal perhaps? To a young Norman who, hopefully would sympathise with Edwina's shy nervousness and lack of confidence.

The brightness of the hall made Edith blink as they stepped through from the passageway. There was a hush and expectant faces turned towards them as they made their respectful curtseys towards the dais. The long tables down the sides of the hall which had often held Saxon lords, friends of her father and brothers, were now filled with Normans.

Although Edith noted some sympathetic glances with a faint sense of surprise, the expressions for the most part were wary; assessing; weighing the girls' value in terms of possible wealth and alliances. These men had come to carve lands for themselves out of the rich soil of England. If blood was spilled in the process – men's or maiden's – what matter? One could always use the new wealth to pay a priest to mutter prayers for salvation. Forgiveness was cheap when balanced against the gain.

Edith raised her eyes at the sound of her father's voice introducing his daughters to the Norman lords.

"My lords, this is my eldest daughter Mathild."

Mathild inclined her head but refused to take her gaze from her father, keeping her expression shuttered and calm.

"...and Edith – "

She dipped her head in turn, almost smiling at her father's usual dismissive tone.

"My youngest daughter, Edwina, only just in her twelfth year." Lord Rufus's voice held a note of warning and defence as though he would protect this last born of his children from too sudden a cruel awakening to the world, then his words became brisk as he reeled off the Norman names, with clumsy pronunciation.

"Lord Ralf de Regny — " – the boar – as Edith still thought of him, the tall Norman who had brought William's demands to Sensgarth, now seated at her father's right, his eyes fixed on the graceful form of Mathild at Edith's side.

"Lord Michel du Fourmeils — "

Edith felt as though she had received a blow in the stomach. Her eyes locked with a dark gaze which repelled her with its intensity yet which seemed to draw her heart from her body, fluttering frantically to escape.

She wanted to run – to hide – from what? She did not know. She knew only that suddenly she was aware of being a woman and that her skin had become sensitive to the lightest breath of air. If someone touched her now she would scream with agony. With an effort she tore her eyes away from his to respond to the names of the other knights in Ralf de Regny's company.

The dull red colour crept up her neck and into her face as she acknowledged the other men seated around the hall, then she forced her legs to move and carry her to her own place at the table.

The hand that raised the cup to her lips was trembling but as she felt the warmth of the wine course through her she drew a breath and endeavoured to bring herself under control. Never had Edith experienced such a turbulence of emotion.

Was it fear?

Yes, certainly. No pity in those eyes.

Was it passion?

Surely not.

Edith had never felt passion for or from any man.

The Saxon lords she had met had not thought to snatch a kiss or pay light court to the slim brown girl listening avidly to tales of honour and courage. Edith leaned forward slightly in her seat and risked a sidelong glance at him as he lounged gracefully in his seat at her father's left. The dark eyes met hers once more and she quickly bent her head. Her heart missed a beat. He was not tall but a lazy strength lay in the ease with which he carried his mail. Although the Normans had donned rich surcoats for the meal they still retained their mail shirts — an understandable precaution.

His hair was blonde, cut short about his ears and glinting in the light. Perhaps it was this fairness which made the fathomless black eyes more shocking... Fallen angel's eyes.

Throughout the meal Edith was conscious of their gaze and she picked desultorily at her food. Finally, after what seemed like hours, the meal was over and the air of tension and strain, which had eased somewhat over the basic business of satisfying hunger and thirst, returned. The tables were cleared and Edith's father and Lord Ralf got down to the discussion of terms.

Edith followed her mother and sisters almost reluctantly from the hall, unable to prevent a backwards glance over her shoulder. A glance she quickly regretted as she caught him watching the gentle sway of her hips as she mounted the stairs. She kept her feet from stumbling only with great concentration and a bead of sweat trickled between her shoulder blades. She seemed to feel the very heat of his stare. It was a relief to reach the familiar security of their room and Edith endeavoured to hide any outward show of the confusion within her as Mathild glanced at her a little curiously. The three sisters undressed in silence, even Edwina's usual chatter stilled by the thought of what the morrow may bring.

As they lay restlessly in the great bed which they had shared for so long Edith could not help a strange tingling of anticipation at the thought of those dark eyes assessing her, and she fought the half-formed hope that perhaps the Lord Michel du Fourmeils was seeking a wife.

Michel had been unable to take his eyes off her. Slim and graceful, the torches drew fire from the demure brown braids and her eyes were soft and gentle. His thighs tensed as she looked straight at him and he saw her eyes widen, the pupils dilate, then she blushed and looked away.

He did not hear the names as Lord Rufus introduced them. He only knew that this was the one he wanted for his wife. A thought struck him and he turned to Ralf, but Ralf had eyes only for the taller girl of the three; cool and blonde, she was like an ice maiden. Michel was relieved. It seemed he need not worry that Ralf might also desire the one that Michel had set his heart on. He forced his attention back to his host and then because he had not been listening to the names, had to whisper frantically to Ralf to find out she was called Edith.

He caught her peeking at him several times during the meal and smiled with satisfaction. It seemed she would be an easy conquest.

When the meal was over, the ladies left the room and he watched her as she accompanied her mother and sisters, noting her backward glance and confusion when she was caught. Then the men settled down to the serious aspects of their presence here.

Edith awoke feeling as tired as if she had not slept at all. Her head was still full of dreams of the dark-eyed Norman pursuing her down a long dark corridor which ended only in a blank wall. The strange thing was that in her dream she had felt no fear, merely the stirrings of a trembling excitement which still found an echo in her limbs as she climbed out of the bed.

Lady Beatrice entered their chamber briskly. With obvious intention of making the best of an unavoidable situation she fussed over their appearance as they dressed, then embraced each of the three sisters before shooing them before her down the stairs. Their father and Lord Ralf de Regny were standing by the fireplace when they entered the hall but there was no sign of the Lord du Fourmeils. Despite herself, Edith felt a quiver of disappointment at his absence, then she chided herself for a fool and forced herself to concentrate on her father and the Norman before her.

Lord Rufus cleared his throat and in a few gruffly spoken sentences outlined the agreement reached by himself and the Lord de Regny concerning his daughters' marriage.

"The Lord de Regny has done our house the great honour of offering for the hand in marriage of my daughter Mathild. Although married previously Lord Ralf has been unhappily a widower for some years. This he now intends to rectify."

Lord Ralf looked away in some embarrassment at the stilted speech and his reaction surprised Edith although not the fact that he had offered for Mathild. De Regny had scarcely been able to take his eyes from her sister since the moment he first saw her. She did not look at her sister, however, keeping her eyes dutifully lowered as she listened to her father, so she missed Mathild's reaction to the news. Then...

"My daughter Edith is to be contracted in marriage to the Lord Michel du Fourmeils of Tierand and Quatre Bras..." Edith heard her father's voice as if from a great distance. She had been fooled by the Norman's absence, assuming he had no further part or interest in the proceedings. The one thought now hammering through her brain was... 'Where is he? If we are to marry, where is he?'

She was answered by the slamming of the door behind her and she swirled about to see the Lord du Fourmeils lazily pulling off his gauntlets as he prowled forward into the hall.

It was though they were the only two people in the world. Her colour high, Edith raised her chin and answered his probing glance with defiance, standing her ground as he moved towards her. He raised a sardonic brow, stopping directly in front of her. He lifted his hand and Edith could not stop herself from flinching away as he gently moved a stray strand of hair from her eyes. He caught hold of the smooth braid to prevent her escape. Their eyes locked and it was only her father's embarrassed clearing of his throat that made the Norman turn his attention from her to the others grouped around the hearth.

"Your pardon my lords and my ladies, but my warhorse was creating havoc in your stables, Lord Rufus and it was necessary for me to calm the brute before he killed somebody. I hope I have not missed too much of the proceedings."

His voice was like warm velvet and Edith tried desperately to stiffen the backs of her knees which had turned annoyingly to jelly at the sensual tones. "Damn him!" Dear Lord forgive her for cursing, but she refused to allow him to see the effect he had on her. Edith was aware of his amused glance and knew he was perfectly sure of her reactions to him.

Edith forced her attention back to her father with great difficulty to learn that Edwina was to be betrothed to Lord Ralf's nephew, Richard.

A sensation of relief washed over Edith with a memory of shining chestnut hair, and a smile glinting at a jest from a companion at the meal the previous evening. Her concern for her younger sister eased considerably. Her father concluded his explanation of the arrangements which affected their lives. The Saxon women were dismissed, their feelings over such matters being considered of little or no importance. As Edith moved away however strong fingers took her arm and warm breath caressed her ear as the Norman murmured, "And is my lady content with the peace terms which require her marriage to a Norman foe?"

Edith paused a moment before forcing her voice to remain calm before she answered.

"Sir, it is not for a Saxon maid to question her father's decision over whom she must marry. Were my intended lord cross-eyed and witless, then even so I must rest content if it be my father's wish."

She felt a surge of satisfaction as his eyes widened in disbelief at her words then swallowed a sense of panic at his cool reply.

"I look forward then to a willing wife to warm my bed, sweet Saxon, where I had expected hatred and tears."

Hastily Edith turned away from his mocking gaze to leave the hall with Mathild and Edwina, mounting the stairs to the women's quarters on legs which had some difficulty in carrying her. It was not until they had returned to their chamber that Edith noticed Mathild's chalk-like pallor and heaving breast.

"I shall not...I shall not...I shall not bed with the Norman hog." Mathild choked and hurled herself onto the bed, her shoulders shaking with sobs. Lady Beatrice and Edith rushed to comfort her. All thought of herself flew from Edith's mind as she vainly tried to reason with her distraught sister. Finally it was an unexpected brutality on Lady Beatrice's part which silenced Mathild. A ringing slap on her cheek stopped the tears and a brisk admonition not to be so selfish – to think of the effect on her father and the whole company of Sensgarth should she refuse. Mathild's eyes widened and her lips compressed as she made a visible effort at control. Then she moved to the window and stared bleakly into the distance.

'Thinking of Edward...' mused Edith and felt a surge of compassion for her sister. At least she and Edwina had not felt the stirrings of sweet first love to be cruelly robbed of that sweetness by war and death.

Edith's thoughts turned to her own mariage and she felt bewilderment at the feelings the Norman roused within her, then a surge of anger at his arrogance. No doubt he had but to lift a dark brow to have the Norman ladies flocking round him. Well he would not find this Saxon maid so easy, Edith decided quiveringly.

Lady Beatrice started to chivvy the girls around. The marriages were to take place at Sensgarth as soon as the priest could be ready, and it was this unseemly haste which had angered Edith's father although he had now calmed somewhat in the face of Lord Ralf's explanations of the need for that haste.

The Normans had to make all speed back to their own strongholds with their new wives for it was then necessary for them to journey on to London to swear fealty to William for the lands they now held from him. They wished their wives to be safe in those strongholds, symbols of their authority in the lords' absence.

Throughout the flurry and confusion of their preparations Edith continued to feel a strange sense of bewilderment. She knew nothing of the man who was to her husband. Would he be kind or cruel to her? She shivered and busied herself with the packing. At least they would all be together for some while yet. Edwina would be living with Mathild. Lord Ralf's nephew, and Edwina's betrothed, Richard, was de Regny's squire and marriage would not take place until

Richard had received his knighthood. Time for the two to get to know one another. As for Mathild...Edith felt a sense of helplessness...she would simply have to pray that Lord Ralf would be understanding and patient...no small thing to ask of such a powerful lord.

The preparations were finally completed and it was with a sense of flying from some inevitable doom that Edith sought the gates of Sensgarth the day before the wedding ceremony. Donning a warm jacket over her blue gunna, she pulled on high leather boots and slipped away through the yard and out of the heavy gates, murmuring her destination to Erld the guard, "The woods, Erld. I shall not be gone long."

"Yes lady Edith. I shall watch for you."

Only one other saw her go.

The lone figure on the walls of Sensgarth hold watched for a moment before wrapping his cloak securely about him, then he turned to descend the steps and follow out through the gate upon the path the Saxon maid had taken.

The guard, Erld, watched him go with sombre eyes. He had known all Lord Rufus's daughters since childhood and he was not happy to see the Norman following the path which Edith had taken. Still – by all accounts she was betrothed to the lord and it was not his place to interfere. However, a frown still creased his brow as the Norman disappeared from sight.

Edith wandered for a while with no idea of her direction until finally she climbed a bank of earth and gazed down into a small hollow which promised shelter from the cold wind. Slipping and sliding in the crumbly earth she made her way to the bottom of the slope and looked around for somewhere to seat herself. It was only as she approached a log jutting from the undergrowth that she heard a sound which turned her blood cold with fear. A high pitched squealing followed by the crashing of broken twigs sent her fleeing back to the far side of the now deadly dangerous hollow. The bank however which had crumbled beneath her feet as she had descended, refused to give purchase to her panic-stricken attempts to clamber out. As the grunting and squealing grew louder behind her, Edith turned to face the danger, pressing her back against the earth as though she would disappear into it. Her arms flung wide, she watched in horror as a wild pig came charging out of the brush into the open.

It stopped for a moment and the small short-sighted red eyes glinted with rage as it scented her presence. For one wild moment Edith thought back to her impression of the Lord Ralf as he had delivered William's demands to her father then she screamed and flung herself to one side as the boar charged at her.

As she fell to the ground she heard a shout, then a stream of curses in the Norman tongue and she raised herself dazedly on her hands to stare appalled as the Norman lord faced the furious boar with only his long sword in his hands. As the boar wavered between the helpless body of the girl on the ground and this new invader of his territory, the Lord du Fourmeils shouted again and jabbed his sword towards the enraged animal. Squealing once more with fury, the heavy pig turned and charged straight at the dancing figure of the mailed warrior. As the boar hurtled towards him the Norman dropped swiftly to one knee and using his sword as he would a spear, jabbed the hilt into the ground. The boar impaled itself with a scream on the long blade. Its momentum, however, carried it forward and it crashed into the kneeling figure knocking it back to the ground to lie still. The dead body of the heavy animal pinned the Norman to the floor of the hollow. Silence reigned, and Edith pushed herself slowly and shakily to her feet, her breath coming in long unsteady gasps as she forced herself to approach the two recumbent forms. Dropping to her knees she gave a sob as she saw the rise and fall of his chest as he lay beneath the dead boar, his white face turned to the side, his blonde hair covered in blood.

Frantically now Edith heaved and pulled at the carcass of the animal he had killed until finally it rolled off the lord, the hilt of the sword jutting from its throat up into the sky. She dropped to the side of the Norman once more, leaning over to brush the dirt from his face. In a twinkling she was flat on her back with the grinning Norman on top of her, her hands pinned to the ground, her eyes wide with shock as she gazed into his.

"Your tender care gladdens my heart, my love, but perhaps I would prefer more tangible proof of your thanks for my saving your life. What think you my lady?"

Edith stared up at him, speechless, then as his head came down to hers, she fought, panic-stricken, to free herself. Her ordeal had left her weak, however, and the Norman was strong and easily stilled her threshing body. Almost tenderly his lips captured hers and for one heart-stopping moment the world spun crazily about her. When he lifted his head once more his expression was unreadable, then abruptly he pushed himself to his feet and held out his hand to help her to rise.

"Come my lady, we must return to the hall before they become concerned about our absence. We shall send some men to bring in our kill. At least we shall have fresh meat for our wedding feast on the morrow."

They spoke no more as they made their way back to Sensgarth. Edith stumbled along at her lord's side, his helping hand sending a tingling fire through her veins which she tried desperately to ignore. The Lord du Fourmeils stared ahead, his face expressionless until they entered the hold. An incredulous Ralf met them as they passed through the gates.

"Miche...what — ?"

Lord Ralf's eyes shuttled between the bloodstained Norman and the dishevelled girl at his side, then as Michel briefly explained what had happened, Ralf shouted orders to his men. They swiftly trotted through the gate in the direction Michel had indicated to recover the dead boar and the Norman's long sword.

With a murmured apology Edith removed her arm from Michel's grasp and fled into the hall and up to her chamber to wash and change her torn clothing. To restore some order to both her appearance and her chaotic emotions. To her dismay Mathild was in the room as she entered breathlessly.

"Saints, Edith, what on earth has happened?" exclaimed her sister.

"I was out walking in the woods and encountered a wild boar. Fortunately for me the Norman was on hand to deal with the creature but as you can see I did not escape lightly. Nor did he."

As she spoke Edith wondered for a moment, who the incident had had the most effect on. She pressed her fingers to lips which still tingled from the touch of Michel's mouth.

Mathild, and then Edwina fussed over Edith for the rest of the afternoon and Lady Beatrice made her daughter lie down on the bed to rest until it was time for the evening meal.

Edith dreaded facing the Norman again but he scarcely even glanced at her as she sat with her sisters on the other side of her parents. Only Edwina seemed to act normally during the meal and her chatter covered up the fact that the two older girls spoke scarcely a word throughout the evening.

At last the table was cleared and they were able to escape to their room where they undressed in silence. Even Edwina sensed the disturbance and strain in her sisters. When their mother had blown out the light, Edith and Mathild lay wakeful beside each other in the big bed, their thoughts on the wedding the next day and what could lie in store for both of them after that. Michel, too, lay awake, Ralf snoring heavily beside him. He was confused by his feelings for the young girl who was to be his wife. He knew he wanted her, fiercely, and he had thought she wanted him, but she kept spitting defiance at him. He was not used to female rejection and certainly her lips and her body responded to his every time he held her. He thought of the moment when she had faced the wild boar and he felt sick at what might have happened to her if he had not been there. Then when he had tried a little playful courtship she had fought like a wildcat until he had forced a kiss upon her.

Michel rolled onto his side. Perhaps when they were wed things would be easier between them. She would be more secure and her role as Lady of Tierand would give her more confidence in herself and in him.

On their wedding morning it started to rain. It was not just a shower but a heavy downpour which soaked everyone who ventured out into it. Its effect on the ladies was to weigh down even more their already low spirits.

Mathild readied herself with her face a tragic mask and Edith found herself worrying more over her sister than about her own situation. After all she decided fatalistically, she was aware that the role of a wife was to cement alliances and provide heirs for her lord. Men sought their pleasures with a mistress. She was startled at the sudden rush of jealousy and rage which the thought brought with it. Surely she could not envy his mistress his kisses and the pressure of his strong body? Yet as her mind treacherously recalled the sweetness of his lips on hers she rebelled at the image of another woman in his arms. Her face was flushed with anger at his imagined infidelity as she and Mathild entered the hall side by side to partake in the ceremony which sealed the agreement between the Norman king and their father the Lord Rufus.

The priest at Sensgarth was a pleasant, middle aged man with kindly blue eyes, whom they had known since childhood and as the two sisters approached the dais which had been lain with rich cloths for the ceremony, he smiled at them encouragingly.

Lord Ralf and Michel stood before the priest and although Lord Ralf turned and smiled as he watched Mathild approach, Edith had only the view of Michel's broad back before her.

She blinked away a tear, then swallowed convulsively as he turned and the passion gleaming from his dark eyes brought heat to her cheeks. Her hand in Michel's, she heard the priest's voice through a haze, her replies automatic, sweat beading her upper lip. She put out her tongue to lick it away and felt Michel turn his head and fix his eyes on her mouth. She quickly closed her lips and as the final responses were made she was swept into his arms and his kiss was a brand setting her body alight. When he finally released her she felt bereft, and her swollen bottom lip trembled. She put out her hand but he had turned away giving orders to his men. Vaguely she heard her mother protesting at something and then he was beside her again and she could not understand what he was saying.

Something about leaving.

When?

Now. Immediately.

Impossible!

His jaw set and he grasped her arm and dragged her to one side.

"It is imperative that we leave at once. I have no time to explain to a protesting wife. Just pack your belongings and make all speed to join me." And with that he was gone to enter into an urgent low-voiced discussion with Lord Ralf. Mathild and Edwina followed her fleeing figure to their chamber and once through the door she could not prevent the sobs from shaking her body. It was Mathild's turn now to offer sympathy, and she enfolded Edith in her arms murmuring consolation until the tears ceased. Bravely pulling herself together, Edith turned to help with packing and in a flurry everything was ready. Michel's men heaved the chests down to the yard and the sisters followed breathlessly. Michel's lips tightened for a moment as he watched the chests being loaded onto a baggage cart, then glancing towards Edith he relaxed slightly and moved towards her. Their mother clung to them briefly

before Michel lifted Edith to her horse, taking her ankle in a
painful grip, forcing her to look into his face. His eyes raised to
hers and he murmured, "Forgive me little bird, the fault lies
elswhere."

Then before she could reply he had turned away, and
shouting orders to his men, leapt to the saddle of the rearing
grey destrier. The troops thundered out through the gates.
Michel and Lord Ralf led the band, the ladies to the centre of
the group with a dozen hard-faced Normans about them.

'Perhaps they think we intend to flee them,' thought Edith,
then shook herself and turned in her saddle to raise her arm to
the group at the gates behind them. Her mother stood, a somewhat forlorn figure in the pouring rain next to her husband. A
pang assailed her, then she set her jaw with determination and
resolutely kept her eyes on Michel's back.

The journey was a nightmare from the moment they left.
The heavy rain made a quagmire of the roadways. The baggage wains became mired and stuck in the mud. The horses
slipped and lost their footing. Men and animals alike were wet
through and miserable. The ladies' skirts clung to their legs,
heavy and unmanageable. Added to the misery of the weather
was the constant need for vigilance.

There were still many a marauding band of Saxons who took
every opportunity to attack the Norman foe, if not from
patriotism, then from greed or simply need. Saxon families
made homeless by the fighting banded together to rob and kill
in order to survive.

Lord Ralf and Michel did all they could to ease the girls'
journey, but even they were finding difficulty in managing
their massive warhorses through the mud. The great horses
slipped and snorted and shied. Then two days after leaving
Sensgarth, as Lord Ralf was struggling with his own horse and
Edith's palfrey, his horse slipped and crashed into Edith's
lighter animal and they both went down in the mud, kicking
and threshing. Edith struggled to her feet attempting to wipe
mud from her face and stay out of the way of the murderously
shod hooves. She fell once more and as she pushed the

hair from her eyes she heard an incredible sound. Laughter! Someone was laughing—at her! Her blood boiled and in a sudden surge of frustration and anger she scooped up a great handful of mud and hurled it at the shaking figure of the man on the horse. Full on the helm it caught him, spattering against the heavy nose piece, into his eyes and down his chest. Too late, she realised she had taken out her rage on her lord. He gasped and scrubbed at the clinging muck, then as she turned to flee, hampered by her heavy skirts, he spurred forward and reaching down hauled her across the saddle before him. It was no mean feat for a mailed warrior, coping with a struggling, spitting, mud-spattered female who was also suffering from an access of terror.

"Be still wench, or you'll have us all in the mud again." He admonished, and dealt a resounding buffet to her already sorely abused buttocks with his gauntleted hand. Edith gasped then bit her lip in an effort to control the tears gathering in her eyes. The jolting in her midriff drove the breath from her body as Michel rode forward with her still across his saddle bow like a sack of grain.

At length he hauled his destrier to a stop and putting his hands about her waist, turned her bodily to sit before him. Suddenly afraid of what she might see in the Norman's eyes, Edith bent her head, but he would have none of it, and putting his fingers beneath her chin, he lifted her face.

Even as she realised his intent, his mud-spattered face swooped to hers and the metal nose piece of his helm pressed into her soft cheek as his lips claimed her own. Shock held Edith rigid for a moment, then as his mouth demanded a response, her lips parted instinctively beneath his. Sudden fire coursed through her veins and her hands lifted to his mailed shoulders of their own accord; arms like bands of steel crushed her to him but she heeded not the pain nor the discomfort. The rain continued to soak the entwined couple but they ignored it and it was only a ragged cheer from the Norman troops which penetrated Edith's brain and made her tear herself from Michel's embrace. Her face was crimson. The Norman gave a low, triumphant laugh, then put up his hand and turned her head into his shoulder to spare her blushes.

Commands were shouted in the Norman tongue and once more the train of soldiers, horses, carts and women struggled through the rain and mud towards their destination, Edith carried more comfortably now in du Fourmeil's arms.

When they reached a suitable camping site that evening, Edith was stiff and sore, and as Michel lowered her to the ground she almost fell again in the mud.

"Have a care, my lady, you would not wish to fall once more in the mire. The consequences would be more then we both could manage. I can only apologise for the lack of comfortable accommodation for such gentle maidens." The last words held an inflexion of sarcasm, but biting back an angry retort Edith merely smiled sweetly and sketched a curtsey.

"My lord, your arrangements are more than satisfactory to this humble Saxon maid and I can only hope that our presence does not cause such powerful lords any more inconvenience than is necessary."

For a moment, the Norman seemed to have some difficulty in controlling his features, then inclining his head to Edith, he backed his horse, and turned and moved away to organise the guard for the night.

Edith watched him for a moment, then hurried to help her sisters with their sleeping arrangements. She missed his considering backwards glance over his shoulder. His eyes lingered on the movement of her hips, then taking a breath, he forced himself to concentrate on the positions of the guards.

Neither he nor Edith slept well that night and the blame did not lie solely with the uncomfortable sleeping arrangements.

For almost a week the troops struggled southwards. Where they found no shelter at abbeys or friendly keeps, they camped on the road. The women shared a shelter in one of the baggage wains whilst the men slept on the ground wrapped in their cloaks.

The rain had finally stopped and they had found shelter at a convent where they had at least been able to dry out their belongings. It was in relative comfort, therefore, that they had recommenced their journey, Edith once nore on her own horse. Michel had disappeared with a troop of his own men and Edith tried to persuade herself that she did not miss him.

Edwina sagged with weariness but seemed to be enjoying enough attention from Richard, her betrothed. Mathild had seemed to build a shell around herself and all Lord Ralf's kindness and understanding seemed unable to pierce it. His small close-set eyes were dark with anxiety as Mathild answered all his attempts at conversation with monosyllabic replies.

Edith was beginning to think that they would never reach the end of their journey when at length Michel du Fourmeil's voice answered once again the guards challenge as the camp was set for the night. Edith's heart leapt within her and she quickly sought occupation for her trembling hands. Mathild glanced at her curiously but Edith turned away from the light and started preparing their beds.

Her lord, however, spent the night in urgent conference with Ralf de Regny. Edith fought down her chagrin and tried to tell herself that of course he must concern himself first with their safety on the road; that a mere woman would not even enter his thoughts at this time. But her heart was heavy within her and not even the brave sunshine the following morning could lighten her spirit.

It was only as she went to mount her horse that she felt herself lifted by strong hands, and as she was placed into the saddle she looked down into dark eyes that mocked her as he bowed gracefully and murmured,

"I trust my lady had a good night's rest. The journey has been arduous and full of danger, but you have borne yourself bravely. Today sees the end of your trials." His lips grazed her hand and he was gone to leap to the saddle of his great grey warhorse.

His voice lifted in command, the echo of Lord Ralf, and the cavalcade moved off. Edith's eyes followed his broad back as he spurred forward and she unthinkingly pressed the hand he had kissed to her lips. So far it seemed the three sisters had

come out of the situation with more than they could have
hoped for. Mathild's attitude to Lord Ralf was still a cause for
concern, but surely the older girl would settle down and be
reasonable with her keep and household to order. After all
their father would not have allowed Mathild to remain un-
married in spite of her grief over Edward. He would have
attached her to some Saxon lord from whom he could derive
the most benefit in the match. Mathild's feelings would not
have been considered in the matter. Thus their position was
really no different than it might have been except that the men
were Normans, not Saxons.

So reasoned Edith as their journey reached its final stages. A
turn in the road brought Michel and his men once more into
view and as the two troops converged, the knight reined his
steed to Edith's side. Edith forced herself to meet his gaze
calmly. Her two sisters drew discreetly to one side so that the
two could converse with some semblance of privacy.

"Tell me, my lady, do you look forward to the end of our
journey?" His voice and glance were quizzical and the query
seemed innocent enough, but as Edith drew breath to reply
she saw the gleam of mockery in his expression.

"Indeed my lord, the journey has been tiring and I feel the
need of a bath and a change of garments." Edith forced herself
to answer politely.

"Ah, I hope I can count on such a dutiful lady to help me
disarm and wash the dust from my own weary frame."

His frame did not look very weary, thought Edith, her gaze
straying to his broad shoulders and once again she felt the urge
to hit out, to disturb that insufferable calm.

"My lord I shall do all that a Saxon lady should do for her
lord and master."

His eyebrows shot up in surprise at her tone.

"Methinks I might not be in a fit state to cope with all that
my Saxon lady thinks that she should do for her lord." His
teeth flashed in a grin of pure devilry and he turned his
destrier's head to ride forward to Lord Ralf's side, leaving
Edith gasping with fury. He was insolent.

An abrupt challenge made Edith raise her head to see the heavy gates of a fortified hall looming before them. Lord Ralf and Michel rode forward to reply to the challenge and as they did so the gates swung wide and a small armed force came out at some speed. The soldiers from their own troop surged forward and closed around the ladies but the soldiers from the hall whooped a welcome and an answering cheer came from their own men. They were obviously at their journey's end.

The hall of Runesay was old but large and commodious. The Saxon lord to whom it had belonged had been ailing and his death shortly before Sir Roger had arrived with King William's decree and the small party of Sir Ralf's men had been a blessing to all parties. The Saxons in the holding had no lord to bind their loyalty and Sir Roger appeared to have won them over so far as it was possible to accepting Ralf as their new lord.

Edith felt a flicker of relief as she noticed Mathild staring around her with her first signs of interest since leaving Sensgarth. Her eyes took note of the dust and cobwebs evident around the hall and her lips tightened grimly. Edith almost smiled but caught herself just in time. The inhabitants of Runesay would soon know that they had a new mistress.

Edith gave a start as she felt her arm taken in a light hold.

"Madame, do you not wish to refresh yourself before the meal?"

Edith turned and looked up into Michel's face. Her blood rose but his expression was serious and preoccupied. Sensing that his thoughts were not on her she nodded her agreement and he led her to the stairs rising from the rear of the hall to an upper floor. Mathild and Edwina followed at his nod and when they reached the top of the stairs Lord Ralf appeared to conduct them to their rooms. Edith left Michel's side reluctantly and entered the small cheerless chamber assigned to her and Edwina. Mathild was offered Lord Ralf's arm and with a blush she laid her fingers upon it and her lord led her away to their own chamber further along.

A knock at the entrance behind them made Edith and Edwina turn to see two servants struggling in with Edwina's chests.

"My lady, which of your boxes do you require for this evening?" panted one of the men to Edith. She raised her brows at the implication that they would not be staying long at Runesay, then she smiled and gave clear instructions to the men.

A quick wash and tidy up and the two sisters were ready to go down as Mathild came into their room to accompany them, her face a little flushed and her eyes bright. The older girl led the descent to the hall, and Lord Ralf came to lead his wife to her place. Her eyes searched the close set gaze of her Norman, then she took a breath and held her head high as she was seated.

Edith was guided to a place at Lord Ralf's other side, Edwina next to her. Her breath caught in excitement as a graceful figure slid into the empty chair between her and Lord Ralf.

Michel did not speak, simply leaned forward to choose bread from the board. Edith was puzzled at his silence, then plucked up her courage and placed her hand on his arm.

"My lord, I never did thank you for your brave actions in the woods at Sensgarth. Please forgive me for being so remiss in my gratitude. I..." Her voice tailed away as his eyes met hers with a glint of anger.

"And would any lord not do the same for his intended wife, and more?" he growled, his usual velvety voice rough and his lips tight. Edith's eyes fell to those lips and her voice was weak as she replied.

" Indeed yes,...I do not know...I did but seek to let you know of my appreciation." Again her voice tailed away—his eyes now were on her mouth and as she put out her tongue to moisten her lips he drew in his breath sharply.

"Don't," he groaned. "As you value your modesty, . . . eat, or I shall not be responsible for my actions."

Edith turned to her platter, a small surge of triumph warming her throat. So! Perhaps there is no love as yet, but there is desire. Oh, yes, there is most certainly desire.

Edith relaxed as the meal progressed. Michel helped her to the tenderest of the meat and shared his cup of wine with her. Each time his hand met hers she felt a tremor run through her.

'Lord help me' she thought, 'If this man loves me not then I am lost, for it would be so easy to give in to this yearning my body has for his.'

She was grateful when the meal was over and the ladies rose to retire from the hall, Mathild's face was fiery as she avoided Lord Ralf's gaze and she gestured to Edith and Edwina to follow her as she left.

As Edith pased Michel he caught her hand and tugged her towards him so that she was forced to bend to listen to him as he spoke to her.

"We must leave at first light. Can you be ready?"

That was all. A brief command. Edith jerked a nod, desperate to escape his nearness which was making her head spin. Before he released her, however he turned her hand and pressed his lips to the inside of her wrist.

"Sleep well my lady. I regret I cannot share your bed this night. I would not wish to make Edwina blush, and so we must wait until we reach our own hall."

Snatching her hand away with an exclamation, Edith hurried past him followed by his short derisive laugh, her breathing ragged and uneven.

When she reached her room she disrobed quickly and silently, avoiding Edwina's curious eyes, cursing the insolent lord beneath her breath.

She slept badly and awoke dull and heavy eyed, the day starting badly as her lord ignored her entrance into the hall. Hurridly swallowing some bread and cheese, washed down with a mouthful of sour ale, Edith was ready as the men collected her small chest and pushed it onto one of the carts.

Edith thanked them a little nervously then hastily embraced and kissed her sisters as her lord fidgeted impatiently on his horse. Lord Ralf lifted her to her saddle and waved farewell as the company cantered out through the gates of Runesay, Edith fighting the lump in her throat. Suddenly her lord turned his head to her and his teeth flashed in a brief smile of encouragement. Absurdly her spirits lifted and she raised her face to the sun as the troop cantered steadily along.

They rode hard all day and Edith was sagging in her saddle with fatigue when Michel finally held up his arm and pulled the troop to a halt. A brief whispered conference with his knights, then he turned his horse towards Edith. His face too was grey and weary, the incredible eyes like black coals as they bored into hers.

"We shall be moving with more caution now," he said grimly, "You are to stay with Arnaud and his men and heed his commands as though they were my own."

She simply nodded, although the questions were fighting for release from her tongue. Michel wheeled away and the troop moved off again, their horses held to a walk, their mail and weapons padded to make as little noise as possible.

As they approached a rise in the land Edith was able to discern a faint clamour in the distance. It was only as they topped the rise and looked down into the small valley below that Edith gasped and the Norman soldiers about her moved into action. They freed their weapons from the muffling cloths and checked their mail before grouping themselves into four companies of very professional and very deadly looking fighting men.

Edith was just able to take in a jumbled scene of fighting; a stronghold under attack, the gates flung wide and several buildings burning. Then Arnaud grasped her bridle and her troop of men hustled her to a small copse of trees to one side of the rise. The rest of the company had spread into a crescent shape along the crest of the hill. Four deep, they readied their weapons and at a word from du Fourmeils they spurred their horses and swept down on the battle below. Edith's hand tightened involuntarily on her bridle making her palfrey dance, and Arnaud leaned over to place a scarred fist on her hand.

"Fear not, my lady, my lord is not one to be easily defeated."

Edith smiled at him gratefully, then turned her eyes once more to the scene below. Michel's men uttered no war cry as they thundered forward. Their faces were grim and deadly beneath the conical Norman helms and the enemy did not even realise their danger until the heavily armed force crashed into them.

Edith, watching anxiously, chewed at her lip with fear as she saw Michel in the thick of the fighting, engaged by a tall, heavily built warrior, riding a black horse. The heavy swords rose and fell as the two hacked fiercely at each other, but although Michel was the smaller and lighter of the two, he was fitter and not so clumsy as his larger opponent, It was soon obvious that, in spite of his size the enemy knight was no match for Edith's lord.

Suddenly Michel's destrier went down, hamstrung by a man on the ground. Michel fell heavily beneath the threshing hooves and Edith rose in her stirrups with a scream. Both hands flew to her mouth and then without further thought she wrenched her horse's bridle from Arnaud's grip, clapping her heels to its side and urging it down into the battle.

After an instant's surprise, Arnaud and his men thundered after her, knowing their lives not worth a groat should anything happen to their lady.

Michel's men had by now realised that their lord was down and were frantically trying to fight their way towards him. Two serjeants were slain; hewn down between the sword of the enemy knight as they tried to protect their fallen lord, and as his opponent dismounted and moved towards him, Michel tried to pull himself clear of his dying horse.

It was the incredible sight of his wife, eyes blazing in her white face, skirts billowing around her, charging straight at his adversary which made his jaw drop open and all his attempts to free himself, cease.

Following the direction of Michel's disbelieving gaze, the approaching knight turned and the shoulder of Edith's horse crashed into him, one iron-shod hoof mashing his face to an unrecognisable, bloody pulp as he went down.

Edith almost fell from the saddle as her horse went over the knight's body but she reined back hard and turned sharply towards where her lord still lay, his furious eyes glaring from beneath his helm.

"Get that damned wench away from here," raged Michel at Arnaud, "Get her away...away."

Edith pulled her horse alongside Arnaud, and ignoring her lord said calmly to the Norman serjeant,

"Come Arnaud, the air becomes somewhat stifling here, it is fresher on the hill."

Leaving Michel opening and closing his mouth like a stranded fish and the serjeant trying vainly to muffle a grin, Edith cantered back to her position on the hill. Her legs were like jelly, her right side was numb where she had crashed into the enemy knight and her lips quivered in an effort to control the weak rush of tears.

'Oh Lord! Michel was furious with her. He would surely beat her black and blue.'

She glanced sideways at Arnaud who raised his brows and then shrugged as if to say, 'Well you brought it upon yourself.'

Bt the time they reached the brow of the hill, Michel's men were mopping up the last dregs of resistance and Michel was astride a captured horse. He gathered his soldiers about him and turned towards the open gates of the stronghold. One man spurred his horse towards Edith and Arnaud and gasped out du Fourmeils' message to his wife. ·

"My lord's compliments and you are to follow to the hall with great caution."

The command was brief with emphasis on the last two words.

Arnaud pressed his lips together although Edith thought she could detect amusement lurking in the corners of his dark eyes. However she simply hunched a shoulder at him and kneed her horse forward at a sedate trot towards the hall that was to be her new home.

The scene which met Edith's gaze as they rode through the gates of the hold almost made her retch. Bodies were flung around like broken dolls. The limbs of one woman were twisted grotesquely as she lay against the wall, her bloodstained skirts in a bundle around her waist.

There was no sign of Michel in the courtyard, although his squire Ranulf was there to assist Edith as she dismounted. As she entered the hall she saw her lord seated at a long heavy table. There was no dais but the table was very ornate with richly carved legs. The chair in which Michel was seated was also heavily carved and the wall behind him was hung with a richly worked tapestry. Before him stood a small group of men, two of whom had obviously suffered wounds. Their leather hauberks were covered with blood and they leaned on their companions. Michel's face was expressionless, only his eyes once again held the cruelty which she had glimpsed when they had first met.

"You say the gates were opened from within," he grated, "You protest that you are blameless and that you did all you could to defend my hall?...I say that I hold you all to account for the death and destruction I see about me. How much were you paid to open to Saer's men?"

The grizzled veteran at the front of the group drew himself up before his lord and answered.

"My lord, I have served you well and faithfully for many years. Why should I betray you now and to such a wolf as Saer de Friese? I say the gates were opened by a traitor, certainly, but not one of our own men."

Michel made an impatient gesture with his hand.

"I shall listen to no more excuses. I shall have no traitors amongst my men. If I cannot find out which of you opened the gates, then all will die. I cannot take the chance of missing the cur who betrayed me."

Edith made a movement of protest and her voice came out as a squeak...

"No... please."

Michel looked up and scowled to see her there.

"What... do you interfere again Madame?" he queried icily, "It seems I am not my own man any more, but must bend and scrape to the lady's whim."

Edith hurried forward and threw herself at her lords's feet.

"My lord you cannot mean what you say. By all means confine the men until you have made an effort to find the culprit, but you cannot slay innocent men, men who have fought and spilled their blood for you, simply because you can't be bothered trying to discover the truth."

Her voice changed from appeal to scorn as she stared into his unrelenting gaze. They stayed so for the space of a heartbeat. Then...

"Well," sighed her husband, "I thought I had me a little brown bird, but the sparrow has turned into a falcon with talons to snatch at my heart."

Edith's breath caught at the last few words but he turned away from her, and gestured to his men.

"It seems, Gerd that you and your men owe your lady more than you can repay." His look turned to Edith.

"I give you my word that no one will die until we have the truth of this matter."

Edith swayed and closed her eyes. Then to her lord's consternation she crumpled in a heap at his feet. Ranulf darted forward to her. Someone was there before him, and Edith felt herself swept up into strong arms before her senses left her completely. The strains of the last few days had suddenly taken their toll.

The long journey and the emotional strain had had its effect on Edith. She slept until late the following morning, and her only memories of the previous night were a confused jumble of gentle hands undressing her, and light kisses pressed to her eyes before she plunged into an exhausted slumber.

She awoke to the sound of shouts and the clash of arms. Alarm raced through her and she struggled from the very large, comfortable bed in which she had slept, to run to the window in her shift. As she leaned out to view the scene below, her glossy brown tresses blew forward and streamed like a banner for all to see in the brisk morning air.

Her husband looked up as he rode into the courtyard, and sat transfixed at the sight of his wife and lady hanging from a window in a gaping shift for all to see. Spitting an oath, he almost fell from his horse and took the steps to the hall in one leap. Edith withdrew herself hastily from the window and dived for the bed, pulling the fur covers around her as high as she could.

The door crashed back on its hinges and the furious Norman took a breath to blast the saucy wench. However the sight of large frightened brown eyes, small hands clutching furs to her breast and unruly brown curls all awry about her face sent the breath from him in a rush. Instead of the tirade she expected, he merely said lamely,

"Madame I have brought you a girl to act as maid and servant for you. I apologise for my lack of consideration in not providing you with someone before this."

And turning he left the room, closing the door behind him. Once outside he leaned back and cursed himself for all the idiots under the sun. He was in the right. He should have beaten her for such unseemly behaviour. But the fear in those eyes...!

He must really be more firm with her in the future.

A memory of the slim body in his arms as he carried her to bed and undressed her the night before made him grit his teeth.

'By the Christ; but he could scarcely make love to an unconscious woman.' A grin split his features. Tonight however! She would be rested and he would woo her this day, so that his lady falcon came to him as indeed the falcon does to the lure.

Thoroughly pleased with himself now he strode down the stairs whistling a merry tune and causing Ranulph and Arnaud to stare and shrug to each other in perplexity. This lady had a strange effect on the lord. he rushed in, boiling mad, forgetting his men, and within a few minutes returned, in love with the world. And he had not even bedded her yet.

A knock at the door made Edith jump, but no one entered until a few moments later, when the door inched open and a freckled, snub-nosed countenance peered timidly around the edge. Her eyes met Edith's and widened slightly, then she stepped into the room and made a fair attempt at a curtsey.

"My lady, the Norman sent me to you. My name is Thrya, and I would be most honoured to serve you."

Thrya gaped as the effect of her Saxon words was to make the Lady Edith throw up her hands and burst into noisy tears.

A rush of sympathy sent her to Edith's side and wrapping comforting arms about her, crooned, "There, my lady, there, the Norman swine shall not touch you, I promise."

Edith suddenly started laughing wildly, and Thrya recoiled — 'Poor lady, her trials had sent her mad.'

'Oh God! thought Edith, the trouble is I *want* the Norman swine to touch me. I burn for him, I yearn for him, yet also I fear his possession. It is well known that men grow cool once they have had their way, and I could not bear it. How on earth Thrya thought that she could prevent Michel from touching her anyway was a mystery, but Edith appreciated the sentiment. It was at this point that she noticed Thyra's thunderstruck expression and she made an effort to pull herself together.

"Thrya. If you would go and organise some food, and some water to wash with, we shall explore my new home together."

Thrya rose hastily to do as Edith bid, thinking that she had best humour her lady at all times. Besides she was more than grateful for her position. She was determined not to return to scrubbing pots in the kitchens. The Saxon maidservant enjoyed her trip to her former working place. In as near an imitation of her mistress's tone as she could manage, she gave Edith's orders with great delight. Her former workmates gaped and scowled but nevertheless hurried to provide the things she asked for. The Lord Michel made his presence felt even in the kitchens.

As Edith broke her fast she eyed Thrya's greasy clothing and red hands with some distaste. Careful questioning confirmed her suspicions as to Thrya's former occupation, but she liked the girl and decided to take her in hand. When she had washed and dressed, Edith opened the chest containing her belongings, which had been brought up and placed at the foot of her bed whilst she slept. Rummaging through the things she had brought from Sensgarth, she pulled out a blue gunna which, although by no means new, would still look well on Thrya. They were much of a size.

First she made Thrya wash as completely as she could, deciding that they all needed a bath. She would arrange for water to be heated. Then as Thrya dressed in the blue gunna Edith rolled the old clothes into a bundle ready for burning.

The two Saxon women looked at each other and smiled. Rapport had been established. Edith led the way from the room and the two set about exploring Edith's new home.

The hall was very old but very solidly built. The upper chambers ran in a semi-circle to the rear of the great hall. The main chamber which Edith had occupied and which she would share with her lord, was at the centre with two smaller rooms at each side. A corridor ran from the back of the hall to the kitchens, which had been built separately to avoid the risk of fire. The great hall itself was very large, much larger than her father's hall at Sensgarth. The fireplace at one side was built of stone, another unusual feature. Carved into the upright at each side of the fireplace was a falcon's head, a fact which made Edith pause and remember Michel's words of the previous day.

As if her thoughts had summoned him, the Norman strode through the door, drawing his gauntlets from his hands and wiping the dust from his face. Edith signed to a servant who hurried away to fetch his lord something to drink. Michel's eyebrows rose at this quick evidence of her authority, but he said nothing, merely seated himself in one of the heavy chairs by the fireplace and started to loosen his mail.

"Allow me, my lord," murmured Edith, reaching to the laces at his throat, but Michel captured her fingers in his and carried them to his lips, observing with interest the becoming blush which suffused her cheeks. He released her hand and the bright dark eyes regarded her expectantly.

Taking a breath, Edith once more attempted to unfasten the ties which laced his mail hood, but by now her fingers were trembling so much that she could not complete the task and as the servant entered with refreshments she snatched her hands away and turned gratefully to the tray set with mugs of ale.

"It seems I have not recovered from my journey," she stammered. "My fingers will not do my will."

She thought she heard a choked laugh from behind her, but when she turned abruptly, her lord was innocently regarding the ceiling. She pressed her lips together and carried him his ale, sipping thoughtfully at her own mug as he drained the liquid thirstily.

Michel stared into the bottom of his mug for a moment before looking up at her piercingly.

"We caught some of Saer's men this morning," he said suddenly, "I should like you to come with me to see them."

"Saer?" she questioned.

Michel sighed.

"Saer is my mother's cousin," he began, "Both my parents are dead and Saer covets everything that is mine, including this hall. "Oh yes," as she showed her surprise, "This hall was my grandfather's hall. My grandmother was a Norman, as was my father, but my grandsire was as Saxon as yourself little bird. Saer is Norman, and he thinks to claim this holding because of my Saxon blood, before I can see William and have my right confirmed. However William now seeks to placate the Saxon lords, and consolidate his rights peacefully. Saer does not know I have myself a Saxon wife on William's orders, and I think he will be shocked when we travel to court, Ralf and I, to swear fealty to William for our lands.

Edith stared at him, one phrase ringing in her ears... " — a Saxon wife on William's orders."... a political pawn, a piece in the Norman's game of power.

Well, what had she expected? How many women were fortunate enough to bed with love when they married?

Edith bit back a sob. She would guard her heart well from this Norman's eyes. She would not let him know his power over her. A dutiful wife he wanted, a dutiful wife he would get.

Michel seemed not to notice Edith's agitation as he led her to the door. His mind was on his prisoners and the information he could extract from them. Saer's men were obviously terrified as Michel approached them.

"I have spared your tender heart the sight of their persuasion," he murmured. "They will be only too ready to tell me who opened my gates to them."

The prisoners had obviously been questioned thoroughly,

judging by the marks on their faces. They hung their heads and stared abjectly at the ground. Michel stood before one serjeant, indolently toying with the clasp of his sword belt.

"I wish to know who played the traitor in my hold, and opened the gates to your men. I trust you understand your position and are prepared to give me some sensible answers."

The serjeant raised his head, and staring defeatedly at Michel, opened his mouth to answer. Before he could do so, however, a shout went up from the gate. All eyes had been for the prisoners and the man Michel sought had seized the opportunity to make his escape.

Michel and his men rushed for the ramparts, his archers stringing their bows.

"A fistful of gold for the man who brings him down." He shouted furiously. Within seconds of his words three goose-feathered shafts protruded from the fleeing man's back and he flung up his arms and fell face downwards. Arnaud, the serjeant noted the successful archers and the company filed back down into the courtyard. Edith was still standing where he had left her and as Michel turned to give the sentence of death to Saer's captured men, he caught her beseeching gaze. They stared into each other'seyes but in spite of her obvious distress, Edith made no murmur against her lord's decision.

'Damn the wench' he thought 'They will think me soft if I spare them, I cannot afford these womanish ways.'

Nevertheless he sighed and turned to the prisoners.

"You are aware of what your fate should be?" he questioned.

"Yes lord." One man forced the answer through dry lips.

"Then you will be doubly grateful for your good fortune when I say that in honour of my lady wife, and to spare her even one moment of sorrow for the death of such miserable knaves, I will instead accept your oath of fealty, not to myself, but to the Lady Edith du Fourmeils."

Edith was as shocked as the six captured men. They fell to their knees and after a moment's hesitation, Edith too bowed her knee before her lord. Michel took her hand and raised her, then kept her fingers grasped in his as the six men swore to honour and defend her until their death.

Edith accepted their oaths gracefully and the men were escorted away to have their wounds bathed and their stomachs filled. Dazedly they followed Arnaud, hardly able to believe their heads were still on their shoulders.

That evening Edith ordered the fire in their chamber to be built up, and servants struggled up the stairs with a large wooden tub and buckets of hot water. Edith sank gratefully into the tub and Thyra added a drop of precious scented oil to the suds. The two girls giggled and splashed until Thrya was almost as wet as her mistress and pools of water lay on the chamber floor. Edith's long brown hair was washed and carefully pinned on top of her head out of the way. It was as Edith rose from her bath and reached for the cloth held for her by Thrya , that the door opened suddenly and Michel pushed his way past the frantically explaining Saxon servant. He stood transfixed at the sight of his wife's slim naked figure gilded rosily by the firelight. Then Thrya quickly whipped the enveloping cloth around her mistress, and Michel's face turned crimson.

"Your pardon Madame," he whispered hoarsely, "I did not understand why the churl sought to prevent me entering my own chamber."

"My lord I did not seek to keep you out. Indeed if you but give me time to dress, I shall be happy to disarm you, and see to your bath."

"No ! I mean, please do not trouble yourself. I shall return when you have finished. Ranulf shall see to my needs. My thanks lady." And Michel strode from the room in great haste.

Edith stared after him open–mouthed for a moment, then slowly a smile curved her lips and catching Thyra's eye the two girls started to choke with laughter.

Michel's men stared as he strode cursing to the stables, shouting for Ranulf his squire. When Ranulf came running at his master's shout, Michel sent him to bring buckets of cold water.

Then, in the stables, the Norman warrior stripped, and with only the horses to witness proof of his desire for Edith, he poured bucket after bucket of icy water over his shivering frame until he had cleansed himself of sweat and dirt, and also controlled his clamouring body.

Edith meanwhile had dressed, and Thrya and the other servants had mopped and tidied the chamber. Descending the stairs to see to having water heated for Michel's bath Edith was dumbstruck by the sight of her shivering dripping lord wrapped only in his cloak, striding across the hall towards her. His stony gaze and tight lips kept her quiet and kept the grins from the faces of the servants as he leaped up the stairs, and the chamber door closed behind him and his squire with a bang.

Turning to the hall, Edith, keeping her face straight with difficulty, and her manner calm, saw to the order of the meal and was seated in her chair at the table when Michel came down, dressed now and in control.

The meal was a light–hearted affair, The men swapped stories of battles and love affairs and Lady Edith's men, now accepted into Arnaud's troop, vied with Gerd and his men in toasting their Saxon lady.

At length, as the platters were cleared from the board, Michel, who had scarcely spoken to Edith, rose to speak to the assembled company; "Men of Tierand, you have all borne witness to my lady's compassion as well as her courage and her impulsive nature.

A small cheer arose, and tankards banged upon the table top. "I now wish to show my appreciation for her sudden method of saving my life, and to honour her bruises for my sake, of which I am sure she has many." Edith, rooted to her chair with surprise, struggled to smile graciously. "Ranulf?"

The squire had slipped out at a whispered command from Michel and now he returned carrying a small doeskin bag. Michel took the bag and tipped it on end. There poured onto the table the shimmering iced fire of a magnificent pearl necklace. It lay on the table like a milky snake as the company stared at it breathlessly. The Michel gathered it in his hands and turning to Edith placed it around her neck. Her soft brown eyes looked into his darker ones and she tried to read the expression in their depth as the Norman soldiers raised the roof of the hall with their cheers.

"I had meant to give you this as my bride gift but I had not the chance, being too occupied with Saer and his men, I hope you forgive me."

Edith could only nod like an idiot.

Her lord took her hand and the two left the table and ascended the stairs to their chamber, their first night together since their marriage. Michel leaned against the closed door as he watched Edith walk across the room before him, her hips swaying gently. He felt strangely nervous before this slim Saxon maid and was therefore at something of a loss as to how to approach her. She did, after all, consider him as enemy — yet she had saved his life by her gallant though foolish action the day before. His breath caught in his throat as she raised her arms and slowly unpinned her hair. The scent of lavender reached him and in two strides he was across the room and had enfolded her in his arms.

Edith looked up into his eyes as his gaze hungrily ravished her face, then her lids fluttered closed as his mouth descended fiercely to hers. Cruel and demanding at first, as she responded his lips eased their punishment and wooed her into surrender.

Michel had cast aside his mail and donned soft rich clothing for the evening meal.

Edith could feel the strength of his desire for her as his arms crushed her to him. Passion engulfed her and her arms twined around his neck as she strained closer to her lord. The contact was unsatisfactory to both of them and breaking their embrace, Michel swiftly disrobed and turned to help Edith with her dress. Her eyes widened with shock as she took her first look at the magnificent frame of her Norman warrior.

Muscles banded his chest and stomach and lean hips tapered to long strong legs. Scars seamed his body here and there from past battles and the whole of one thigh was discoloured with bruises where he had gone down beneath his horse the previous day.

"Edith?" he whispered, and her eyes flew to his. Then she turned from him as he moved towards her. Slowly he undressed her until she was clad only in the gift of his necklace. Unable to contain his desire any longer, he lifted her and moved to the great bed. Shivers shook her body as he laid her down, but it was not that she was cold. A strange sense of excitement and anticipation gripped her, and her heart pounded in her ears as he stretched his lean and powerful frame next to her. His eyes feasted on the treasure before him and she turned on her side towards him, partly to shield her nakedness from his hungry gaze, and partly to share the warmth emanating from his body.

His mouth caressed her temple then slid down her cheek and to her throat. There he lingered a moment before tasting the soft skin of her shoulder. His hand came up and pushed her on to her back his lips leaving a trail of fire from her shoulder to her breast. She turned her head and fastened her mouth to the only part of his body she could reach and as he felt her lips against the muscles of his upper arm, his control snapped and his weight came full upon her.

Inevitably he hurt her. His urgency was too great, and as she cried out in her pain, he whispered his remorse in her ear, kissing the great crystal tears from her cheeks.

"The pain grows less little falcon, I promise," he murmured. Her answer was to turn her mouth up to his and cling to his powerful shoulders as he loomed above her.

8

The following weeks were weeks of pure undiluted happiness for Edith. The Norman lord and his Saxon lady seemed content with each other. As the weather improved Michel looked to his defences. A new palisade was erected around the hall, this time higher and thicker, on top of a great bank of earth. On the outside of the wall the serfs laboured at a great ditch. Michel was only satisfied with it when it was necessary to use ladders to climb out from the bottom. He then had his men prepare long wooden stakes and these he planted at an angle in the bottom of his ditch with the ends jutting up into the air, sharpened like lances. As well as the great double gates they constructed a drawbridge, the underside of which was also studded with sharpened stakes. Tierand hall then fairly bristled with defences. It would take a formidable enemy to conquer this lord.

Edith too was busy. She cleared out all the old rushes and mixing great vats of lime, she had the hall servants scrubbing and washing and disinfecting the hall from top to bottom. The linens were washed and laid out in the spring sunshine to dry until finally Tierand smelled as sweet as the spring flowers. Thrya brought Edith two more girls, suitably scrubbed and dressed, who were good with their needles and the four women set to spinning, weaving and sewing until their fingers ached and their eyes smarted. The great table and carved chairs in the hall were polished with lavender and beeswax and beautiful tapestries woven by Michel's Norman grandmother were dusted and carefully aired until the bright colours gleamed through once more.

Then three and half weeks after their return to Tierand, Michel and Edith were taking their meal in the hall when the drawbridge rumbled up, the gates swung to and the sentry shouted a challenge.

Michel threw down his cup and with his mouth full of meat, shouted for his weapons as he ran from the hall.

Edith's heart was in her mouth until she heard the drawbridge rattling down once more and she hurried to the door to see who had caused the commotion. Once there she gave a shriek of joy and lifting her skirts, flew down the steps to fling her arms around Mathild and Edwina in turn. The three sisters all tried to talk at the same time until Lord Ralf's amused voice broke in upon their gabble.

"Well Michel, a fine lady this who does not offer weary guests even a cupful of ale to wash the dust from their throats. Lady Edith are we to sleep in the ward tonight or will you not invite us in?"

Overcome by her lack of manners but pleading her joy as an excuse, she led the visitors into the hall, sending servants for food and drink and drawing Mathild and Edwina to sit.

"Marriage seems to agree with you." dryly noted Mathild, eyeing Edith's flushed cheeks and sparkling eyes.

"I have no complaint," murmured Edith somewhat shyly, "And you? Do you fare well?"

"My lord is kindness itself and one must make the best of what one has. He is not the hog I thought him. His looks belie the truth."

Edith turned to Edwina.

"And how like you being betrothed to Richard?"

Edwina's smile lit up her face.

"My Richard is good and brave. He makes me laugh so much sometimes my stomach aches. I am more than content."

Thus assured that all was well with each other, the sisters settled themselves to talk of more mundane matters.

As Edith has guessed, Mathild had turned Runesay upside down to bring the cleanliness and standards of service up to her own high requirements. They laughed over stories of evicted vermin sending screaming serving girls up on to chairs and other places which they deemed out of reach of sharp teeth and scaly claws.

Edith responded with Thrya's reaction to her mistress's attack of hysterics at their first meeting. As they laughed and chattered Edith glanced towards her lord where he stood in earnest conversation with Lord Ralf. With foreboding she saw his lips tighten grimly and his eyes narrow into the cruel lines she had once feared so much.

Mathild paused in her conversation, looking also to her lord as she noticed Edith's abstraction.

"We heard of your trouble", she said, "That was the reason for your lord's haste on the marriage day."

"Yes," Edith replied, "He talks of a journey to William's court to swear for the lands."

Mathild nodded. "Ralf has said he must go, and Michel also; this William has a suspicious nature and sees betrayal where none is intended. Do you go with your lord?"

"He has not said, and I have not asked him. We have talked of other things." Edith's eyes fell as she said this and Mathild smiled gently., So that was how things lay? So long as Edith's love was returned – Mathild considered Michel broodingly. A fair Norman – fit to steal the heart of any maid. She envisioned his causing havoc amongst the ladies at William's court. Few men had a true heart. Even Edward, her betrothed Saxon lord... Mathild closed her mind to the thought, which surprisingly did not bring the pain she had expected. She turned as a hand grasped her shoulder, and looked up into the concerned brown eyes of her lord.

"Are you well?" queried Ralf. "You seemed a little pale just now."

"All is well with me my lord, I thank you. It is merely the journey which has tired me somewhat."

"You must rest and enjoy your visit. You have worked hard these last few weeks and the results of your labours are much appreciated...if not by the servants, – most certainly by your lord."

Mathild smiled up into his face.

"I am glad my labours have pleased you my lord. I am only a poor Saxon maid who fears her conqueror."

A slap on the buttocks was Ralf's reply to this sally and Edith regarded the byeplay with delight and considerable satisfaction. It seemed she had no need to worry over Mathild.

The meal that evening was a merry affair. The lords and their knights vied with each other to tell the most outrageous stories, and Richard, Edwina's betrothed, brought out his lute and entertained them all with ballards of love and songs of heroes long gone. He even slipped into one or two bawdy lays which had the soldiers roaring and which the ladies pretended not to understand.

At length tiredness overcame the revellers and even the most enthusiastic sergeant sought his bed. The ladies retired and left their lords in deep discussion of the now urgent trip to court.

"Saer will be pouring poison into William's ear," grated Michel. "He must be stopped one way or another. This attack on my hall was a rash move, but it could well have paid off had the messenger not reached me in time."

"How could he have excused his attack to William?" queried Ralf, "Even Saer would have to think of some good reasons for attacking his own cousin."

"That is what worries me. He would not take the risk if he had not had some reason to think he could get away with it."

"We must delay no longer. I can be ready in a few days. Luckily Tierand is close enough to my own hall that we should have no problem with leaving enough men for the defence of either should they be attacked. You will not take your lady?"

"No. We shall travel faster alone, and I can plead my concern for her as my reason to keep our visit as short as possible. I will say she is nervous and cannot be left too long alone."

"Ah yes," joked Ralf, "I have heard of the lady's timidity and her lack of decision. It must be a sore trial to you to have to deal with her constant weeping and complaining."

The two lords grinned at each other and Michel slapped Lord Ralf on the back.

"Come on then – to bed. We shall tell the ladies of the arrangements in the morning."

When Michel entered their chamber it was to discover Edith asleep in the chair by the dying fire, her head pillowed on her arm. Smiling tenderly he lifted her, and removing her robe, placed her gently on the bed. She did not wake and he undressed quietly and slid into his place at her side. She turned to him in her sleep and he felt the surge of desire in his loins. Fighting down the temptation, however, to wake her and taste of her sweetness, he closed his eyes and the two spent their night wrapped in each other's arms.

When Edith awoke the next mornng, Michel was still asleep and she leaned up on her elbow to study his face as he slept. His brows and lashes were very dark in comparison to his blonde hair which, badly in need of cutting, was starting to curl over his neck and ears. Edith felt a compulsion to slip her fingers into the curls. A thin scar ran across the bridge of his nose, then slanted up over a cheekbone. As though he felt her gaze, his eyelashes fluttered and his eyes opened. Lost, she stared into their bright, dark depths until their expression deepened and his hand slid behind her head and slowly brought her mouth down to his. Passion flared and ran down her body like a flame.

His arm came up and around her shoulders and with a sudden movement he rolled and lay atop her, not breaking the contact with her mouth. Caressing fingers grazed her breasts and she arched her body beneath him. His mouth left hers to travel across her cheekbone to her ear. She murmured his name and his tongue flicked, sending shivers down her spine. No pain now. Just a deep red well of pleasure which swept over her, leaving her gasping and clinging to his broad shoulders as if to a lifeline.

Afterwards they lay entwined and he ran the brown silk of her hair through his fingers, caressingly.

Michel was at a loss, not knowing how to tell her of his imminent departure. He was not usually so reluctant to leave a woman even be it his wife. This little Saxon falcon had her talons well and truly into his heart. Slowly he explained to her the need for haste.

Edith lay regarding him with her soft brown eyes as he spoke.

"And may I not go with you my lord?" she said softly.

"I need to use you as a reason not to stay too long. You will be perfectly safe here. I shall leave you Gerd and his troop, also your own men who swore to you that day. Lord Ralf leaves a full company at Runesay should you need more help. All will be well sweetheart."

She wanted to cry out that she was not afraid, that she simply wanted to be with him. But his use of the word 'sweetheart' closed her throat and she could say nothing. He trusted his hall to her and she would not fail him. She would smile and wave farewell, knowing that if he should not return the light in their life would go out.

The decision made, Lord Ralf left that same day with Mathild and Edwina. In three days he would return with a small company of men and Michel would join him on the road to London taking over two thirds of his own men with him. This left Tierand only lightly manned, but Ruensay was within easy reach and a strong force was still needed when Norman lords were travelling the English roads.

The three days flew by in the welter of preparation. Provisions were readied for the travellers and the holding stores were checked so that should an enemy lay siege to Tierand, there would be sufficient food and weapons to last until help could arrive from Runesay. Michel and his men checked their own armour and weapons and Michel practised on his new mount – a strong young horse which he had been training to replace his much mourned grey, lost in the battle with Saer's men.

Finally the challenge came from the gates and at Lord Ralf's reply, the drawbridge creaked down and the boards echoed hollowly to the thud of the horses' hooves. A pause for a mouthful of food and a draught of ale and Edith stood to bid farewell to her lord in the courtyard. Michel mounted his new destrier with a little difficulty then bending to his wife, he lifted her clear off the ground and his lips clung to hers in a brief farewell. Edith bit her lip and forced a smile as they rode out, then flew up to the walls with Thrya beside her to watch until her lord had vanished from sight. Thrya placed an arm about her shoulders and led her down the steps and into the hall, closing the heavy doors against the cool spring air.

It took Michel and Lord Ralf several days to reach London although they travelled hard and fast. Stopping only to wash and change from their mail into clothes more suitable for court, they left their men quartered at a nearby inn and presented themselves to William.

William's face was unreadable as the two lords bowed before him.

"You have not been over hasty in presenting yourselves to us my lords. We had expected to see you some time before this."

"Your pardon Sire, but it is sometimes difficult for a newly wed husband to explain to his bride why he must leave her only days after the wedding."

Ralf's voice was gruff as he explained.

William's brows arched towards the gold circlet banding his brow.

"You were successful then, in taking the ladies to wife and securing the father's loyalty?"

"Yes Sire, the only drop of blood spilled was spilled by Normans attacking my holding in my absence." Michel allowed a note of bitterness to creep into his voice and he watched Willliam's face carefully.

William however smiled blandly and replied.

"Ah yes. I did hear of some difficulty concerning the claim to your holding. However you are here now and in a few days I shall take your oaths for the lands you hold from me. And now my lords, if you will excuse me – ?"

Michel and Ralf bowed deeply and left the chamber.

They said nothing until they were on their horses and riding back towards the inn.

Michel slid a sidelong glance to Lord Ralf.

"I think, my friend, that it was as well we came when we did. Saer has obviously been pouring his tale of woe into William's ear."

"You must have a care Michel. Look to your arms whilst we are here."

"Aye Ralf. I find myself worrying about our ladies left alone whilst we dance attendance at William's court. I must see if I can discover Saer's whereabouts."

On their return to the inn, Michel and Ralf took Arnaud and one of his men to one side in a whispered conference. Half an hour later two figures slipped from the rear of the inn and were quickly lost to sight amongst the throngs of people going about their business in the London streets.

They did not reappear until the next morning when Michel and Ralf were in the stables checking their horses. Whilst Arnaud and his man changed back from the borrowed rags into their own mail, they gave what was to the two lords a very disturbing report.

The Lord Saer de Friese was no longer in London. He and all his men had left at a hard pace on the morning of Ralf's and Michel's arrival. There was little the two lords could do. To leave with all their men before swearing to William was asking for trouble. William was very touchy at this time and jealous of the honour he considered due to him. However they did what they could. Arnaud and his men, along with Ralf's serjeant Hugo and a small force of Ralf's soldiers were soon mounted and provisioned and after being given the command to 'ride like the wind', they took the road out of London as though the very devil was at their heels.

Michel and Ralf watched the small force depart, then with a sigh turned back into the inn.

"We can do no more. At least there are plenty of men at Runesay should there be a need."

Michel nodded at Ralf's words and gave a feeble attempt at a smile, but his heart sank with foreboding. William had been very off-hand with him and Michel knew that the King liked to keep his lords under his thumb. Was this William's way of reminding them that he was the master and that what they held they held by his favour and his favour alone?

Even their wives they had by William's good grace. At this thought, Michel's mind flew to Edith. She had certainly got under his skin and he found himself reaching out for her in the night, only to touch empty space beside him. It was the first time he had ever actually missed a certain person's presence and he even viewed the local whores with a distaste born of comparison to his wife. He closed his eyes on an image of Edith's face, sheened with the fine sweat of her passion as she moved beneath him. He shook his head and rubbed his hands briskly over his eyes to block out the disturbing vision. Ralf glanced at him curiously but forbore to comment on his friend's drawn looks and worried frown.

"Come Ralf, there is no sense in brooding, and worrying over something about which we can do nothing. Let us taste a little of that which the city of London has to offer two lords with money to spend"

So Michel and Ralf ventured onto the streets of London with plenty of gold in their belts and a small troop of their men to ensure that no-one tried to part them from their gold without giving something in return. After a night of drinking deeply the two lords made their unsteady way back to the inn where they were staying. It was as they turned into the narrow street where the inn stood that dark shadows detached themselves from the wall and swiftly and silently surrounded the small group of Normans. The light glinted on drawn daggers and two of their escort fell to the floor with a dying groan. Michel and Ralf had fortunately donned their mail once more before venturing abroad into the city, and as they realised their danger the two warriors whirled into action, drawing their mighty swords and standing back to back as the killers closed in.

Shouting his battle cry, Michel raised his sword above his head and charged at his attackers. They fell back as they faced a furious, battle-seasoned warrior who had lost count of the times he had dealt with furtive attacks in narrow streets with the odds definitely against him.

Michel felt his blade bite deep with a surge of satisfaction, then he spun around to slice his sword into the arm of a man gliding behind his with dagger raised. Ralf was holding his own, and as the noise and confusion increased, lights flared in the buildings around them. The door of their own hostelry swung open and a vengeful band of troops charged into the street, forcing the remaining attackers to drop their weapons and run for their lives.

Michel and Ralf watched them go, Ralf breathing a little heavily after his exertions.

"I think I am too old for this sort of thing," he gasped ruefully.

"My friend, I would rather have you at my back than half a dozen of any other warrior," laughed Michel slapping his comrade in arms on the shoulder.

"Come, let us to bed, we can examine the bodies in the morning.

And the two lords turned into the yard of the inn to retire for the night. The next morning however, the bodies had vanished from the stables where Ralf's men had laid them. The two Normans were furious, as much with themselves as with their men.

"Damn my carelessness," raged Michel, "If we could have identified their carcasses we might have had something definite about which to complain to William."

"The fault lies with me as much as with you. There is nothing we can do about it now so we may as well forget it and hope that William makes all speed to take our oaths so that we can return home."

But William kept the two knights fretting and fuming; kicking their heels at the inn before finally the summons to court arrived. Tense and on edge with anger and frustration, Michel was hard put to it to keep his feelings from showing before William. As it was, something must have shown in his eyes for William kept his hands between his for much longer that was strictly usual when Michel was taking the oath of fealty. As Michel stepped back after accepting the kiss of peace from the King, William leaned forward and murmured;

"Keep faith with me Lord du Fourmeils, hard though you may find it at times. Look to your lady and your lands and I will find it in my heart to honour you."

Michel bent his knee to his king and left the court with his heart full of anxiety. With the Lord Ralf hard on his heels Michel leaped to his horse and fought his way frantically through the press of people towards the inn. Within the hour the whole company of men who had come to London from Tierand and Runesay were pushing their horses to the limit on the road home.

10

The first few days of Michel's absence were sheer misery for
Edith. She lost her appetite and she could not sleep in the big
bed without her husband beside her. Thyra fussed and fretted
over her until the third morning when Edith decided she must
pull herself together or she would go raving mad before her
lord's return. The weaving was well under way and the pile of
linen for the household was growing. One thing she lacked
was a store of herbs. So with Thyra in close attendance she
descended to the ward and calling Gerd the serjeant to her
asked him to find her a capable man who could start a small
garden for her. She then ordered him to saddle her horse and
also one for Thyra. Her maid protested that she could not ride,
indeed had never been on a horse in her life and if her lady
would excuse her, she would really rather not attempt the
experience. Edith brushed aside her maid's protests and a
quiet old mare was saddled for Thyra. With Gerd and a small
mounted troop of men, Edith set out to explore the area
around the holding. The hall itself was set on top of a hill at the
opposite end of the valley from the point where Edith had
viewed the fighting on the day of her arrival.

Around the base of the hill were the few scattered huts of
the serfs. One hut slightly larger and better built than the rest
proclaimed itself an alehouse by the green hop-bush hanging
from the doorway.

Edith halted outside this door and the alewife came out
bobbing and curtseying, a large beam on her face at the honour
done to her house. With a few well chosen questions Edith
soon had the information she needed and an hour later was
cantering steadily back to the hall with a basket lined with
damp moss and containing quite a wide selection of herbs she
would need for her garden.

After something to eat that afternoon, Edith and Thyra, with
the man Gerd had assigned to be her gardener, chose a shel-
tered spot to the rear of the hall with varying areas of shade
and sun, for her herb garden. The rest of the day was spent
planning and marking out the ground, and in deep discussion
with her gardener. It was essential that herbs were available to
Edith as mistress of the hall, to treat wounds and hurts as well
as for cooking and curing food. At the meal that evening Edith
was tired, and as near to being happy as she could get.

The day had gone by quickly and this suited her. The time
could not go fast enough until Michel was with her again.

For a week after that Edith kept herself busy. The last place
for her inspection was the armoury. Her husband had checked
this before he left, but Edith thought that it would be as well
for her to be familiar with all the means of defence which
would be at her disposal should they be attacked. She must
have been forewarned; they were halfway through this task
when a shout went up from the walls. With a muttered excuse
Gerd ran from Edith's side and with scarcely a second's
hesitation Edith followed him into the yard and then up the
ladder to the walls. When she arrived breathlessly at the top,
Gerd was in earnest conversation with the soldier who had
cried a warning. Edith gazed out over the deserted valley.
Nothing stirred; unless.... A light suddenly winked on the
edge of the woods. Edith caught her breath. The sun on
armour, or the point of a lance? No friend need lurk in the
woods. She turned as Gerd reached her side.

"You saw my lady?"

"Aye Gerd, Summon the men."

All at once the walls swarmed with men. Weapons clanked

and men cursed as they found a position. Gerd ran from man to man urging silence. Every other man down...out of sight...behind the palisade. Edith watched as troops emerged from the woods all along the skyline at the end of the valley. How many? Difficult to say...Too many!

Who was it?

Edith thought she knew. Her heart sank. She must get word to Runesay.

"Gerd...we must send a man to Runesay. We need help."

Almost before the words were out of her mouth two men stood before her, both members of the group for whose lives she had pleaded so eloquently the first day she came to Tierand. "Two men have more chance of getting through than one my lady."

"Very well. Choose different paths. No horses. You must sacrifice speed for stealth. God go with you."

The two men left separately. Lowered by a rope from the wall at the rear of the holding, out of sight of the approaching force.

Edith watched the second man reach cover with a sigh of relief.

How long would it take them to reach Runesay? Three days. Then another day for help to reach them. They must hold out for a least four days.

How? She did not know.

She glanced around the hold. Her defending force was pitifully small, but they were all seasoned warriors and her lord had laboured well and to good effect on Tierand's defences. A loud hail from without the walls interrupted her thoughts. Slowly and with as much dignity as she could muster Edith mounted once more to the wall above the gate.

The enemy was before her.

She paled as she realised the size of the force. Several hundred men. To defeat one woman. Surely Saer had an inflated opinion of her ability. For it was indeed the Lord Saer de Friese. He was impressive to look upon. Taller than her lord and built like a bull, his voice was strangely high pitched for so massive a man.

"Lady Edith due Fourmeils?"

Edith acknowledged him with a curt nod of her head. Gerd loomed beside her protectively, his shield at the ready.

"Lady Edith, in the name of King William, I demand that you surrender this keep and all within it into my hands. If you yield, no man will die. You will be treated with honour. This, I, Saer de Friese, promise on my oath as a Norman knight."

There was a moment of silence as Edith felt the glow of rage building within her.

'His word as a Norman kight' meant nothing to her. Her lord had left her in command of his home and she would defend it to her last breath.

She began; "Sir, I know who you are and what you are, and I know also that anyone with a legal and rightful claim to this hall and these lands would not need to come here in force demanding their surrender. You call on me in William's name. Let me tell you that even if William himself were to come to my gates in force and demand that I yield, I would deny him unless my lord commanded that I open to him."

She then watched as Saer's face turned purple with fury and as he wheeled his charger about she caught his words; "Not yield? We shall see – we shall see.

Then he was gone, thundering back to his men with his squire and knights beside him. Edith took a breath and turned to Gerd. He was regarding her with his mouth hanging slack and somewhat glazed look to his eye.

"Gerd?" she questioned.

Gerd came to himself.

"Yes my lady." Solicitously and with great respect obvious on his face, Gerd escorted her from the walls.

A quarter of an hour, later Saer launched his first attack. In that quarter of an hour, water was heated to boiling point in the laundry tubs. Buckets cooking pots, even old helmets were gathered to carry the boiling water. As well as Edith's women, there were the women from the village who had sought safety within the walls as soon as the first enemy soldiers had been sighted.

Every woman had a weapon...a knife, an axe, the straight tines of a hay fork, anything that would rip at human flesh. Great piles of stones were heaped at various points along the wall and burning pitch bubbled in a pot alongside each group of archers.

Edith was at her post on the wall above the gate when Saer's force began to move. At her side were bow and arrows. Thrust into her belt, a wicked looking knife handed her by a kitchen boy. Her lips pressed into a grim line reminiscent of the Lord Michel.

Saer's men were strangely silent as they advanced. Only the clank of their weapons sounded...not a voice was raised.

Gerd calmly signalled to his archers and evey other man along the wall knocked an arrow to his bow and sighted.

"Take your time and choose your man," called Gerd, then fell silent to watch the on-coming force.

Edith held her breath as the enemy came closer and closer.

She wanted to scream 'Fire! What are you waiting for? Shoot! Shoot!' And as the thought left her mind Gerd's arm came down in the awaited signal.

The air was black with the arc of goose feathered shafts. Edith saw them strike home all along Saer's front line of men. As the first archers bent for another arrow, every second man behind the wall rose with his bowstring pulled back to his ear and another deadly hail hissed towards the attackers. Men were falling like nine-pins, confusion spread, Saer's archers had not even loosed one flight of arrows as the fourth flight of falling death hit his men. The advance stopped. Bodies lay in all directions. Saer bawled a command and with speed it was obeyed as his men moved hastily out of range of Edith's archers.

Gerd grinned at Edith

"One to us my lady. He'll not underestimate us next time."

"That's what worries me Gerd."

As soon as the words were out of her mouth, the enemy had started to advance once more. This time they were split into smaller individual groups...harder to hit...and they

carried their shields so that each man was overlapped by the
shield of the man next to him. Gerd's lips tightened, then he
swung round and moving quickly around the walls gave
careful instructions to each group of archers. The hail of arrows
which flew from the walls of Tierand were now aimed up into
the air and before Saer's men could raise their shields over
their heads in protection the deadly shafts took their toll.
Saer's serjeants roared at the men, urging them on over their
fallen comrades and they were soon crowding along the edges
of Michel's formidable ditch. The front wave of men, pushed
from behind, teetered and fell. The deadly pointed stakes did
their work and the terrible screaming from impaled soldiers
made Edith lose a little colour. Gerd, noting her reaction, told
several archers to silence the dying men and then once more
Saer's men received the order to fall back. Edith's defending
force jeered and catcalled as the enemy scrambled and fought
to get out of range of the deadly arrows which followed them.

Edith relaxed her hands which had been balled into tight
fists at her sides and took a deep, shuddering breath, then she
and Gerd watched as Saer and his men stopped their headlong
flight and the serjeants gathered their men together again.

The knights closed around their lord and after a deep and
earnest consultation, the company set about constructing
defence lines with the obvious intention of settling down to lay
siege to Tierand keep.

"If we can just hold them for a few days, until help comes
from Runesay," murmured Edith to Gerd as she broodingly
watched Saer's preparations. Chewing at her lip she turned
from the walls and motioning to Gerd to accompany her, she
descended the steps and entered the hall. Sending a servant
for something to drink, she seated herself in the chair and
waved to Gerd to sit also.

"Saer's force far outweighs our own and although my lord's
defences are excellently well thought of, we must turn our
minds to more devious means of defeating the enemy."

Gerd's brows rose but he was now almost beyond being
surprised by anything his lady did. She was an unusual

and he was glad it was for the lord to rule her, and all that he had to do was follow orders.

Edith stared into her cup for several minutes, and then slowly, an almost fiendish smile curved her normally sweet mouth.

"If Saer will just hold off until nightfall...", she mused, almost to herself, then she glanced up straight into Gerd's eyes and gave a most delightful chuckle.

A thud and a curse, then a fierce whisper urging silence. Several groups in dark shadows gathered on the edge of the ditch carrying long narrow bundles. Quickly and silently the groups moved towards Saer's encampment. No guards challenged as the darkly clad figures laid their bundles down, and quickly unwrapping the covers, revealed the long ash bows and goose feather tipped arrows.

A spark; a flash of fire, and within seconds, flights of flaming arrows ascended into the skies, their targets...the tents and baggage wagons of Saer's force.

As the fire arrows found their marks, the uproar began. Semi-naked warriors came tumbling from the blazing tents, cursing and shouting. Horses shrieked with fear as the blaze spread and guards challenged their own men or their own shadows in panic.

The culprits from Tierand slipped away as silently as they had arrived and the drawbridge was lowered and the gates opened to welcome them home. Saer's men were too busy to notice. All Michel's men returned safely. Edith and Gerd stood at the walls watching in delight as Saer and his men spent a sleepless night dousing the fires, chasing horses, and attempting to save their precious equipment.

The next morning saw Saer and his knights once more outside Tierand gates to parley. Saer's strange high-pitched voice was raised again to the Lady du Fourmeils.

"So, my lady, you think you have won with your stupid, devious tricks. We shall see how you feel by this evening when your hall is burning around your ears. I call upon you once more to surrender this keep to its rightful lord."

A moment of silence followed this amazing speech, and then an extremely loud and extremely rude noise issued from one of Edith's soldiers.

Stifling an almost irresistable urge to laugh loud and long in Saer's very face, Edith took a breath and answered the Lord du Friese.

"Sir, I earnestly advise you to desist from your foolish efforts to take this stronghold. My lord has laboured long and well at our defences and my warriors are no puling youths to be overset by your threats. I shall most certainly yield to my rightful lord, and only to him...the Lord Michel du Fourmeils, my husband."

For a moment Saer's face had lightened with triumph at Edith's statement of intent to yield, then as the rest of her words penetrated his brain he gave a strangled squawk of fury and wrenched brutally on his horse's bit, sending it up on its hind legs and spinning round to gallop back to what was left of his encampment.

For the rest of that day Edith and Gerd watched Saer's force chop at trees and saplings in the surrounding woods. The sound of busy hammering filled the air as Saer directed the construction of weapons designed to bring about the downfall of Tierand keep.

Gerd's face was grim as by evening the silhouettes of the crude siege weapons stood stark against the sky.

"They will be on their guard against another sortie to destroy their hand-work," he grated as he and Edith once more consulted together in the great hall.

"Hmm, yes. Another attack of that kind is out of the question. We must hold for at least two more days before we can expect any help from Runesay. Make sure that there are

sufficient vessels of water around the keep in case of fire
arrows and check that each of own archers has plenty of
arrows in readiness. More than that we cannot do except trust
in God and in my lord's defences. Pray that the force from
Runesay makes all speed to reach us."

The attack began almost as soon as the sun lighted the
sky the next morning. There were no huge boulders around
Tierand for Saer to use as ammunition but slings full of small
rocks and burning brushwood rained on the defenders. The
hall was turned into a sanctuary for the wounded and burned,
and Edith even tore up her newer robes to make soft cloths to
bind their hurts. Everything inside the keep that was burnable
was thoroughly doused with water, one of the few things in
plentiful supply, as Tierand had a deep well close under the
walls in a fairly protected spot.

This time Saer de Friese was almost gloating with triumph
and wasted little time on the courtesies.

"Well madame and how is your fine defiance now? Not so
proud as before I'll warrant."

Edith clenched her fists before her on the stout walls and her
voice rang with hate as she answered:

"I have given you my answer sir, and nothing you can say or
do will make me change that answer. You are a foul dog who
would betray his kinsman and take all that is his where you
have no right. I do not wish to speak with you again, so you
can save your breath for running when my Lord du Fourmeils
returns to take vengeance for your crime against him."

So saying Edith turned from the walls, paying no heed to the
oaths which beat about her ears as Saer gave vent to his rage.

Once seated in her chair however, Edith raised trembling
hands to cover her face. Gerd sent a servant scurrying for wine
and held Edith's cup to her to drink.

"My lady, you must rest. Saer can do nothing tonight and
tomorrow should see succour from Runesay. You do neither
yourself nor us any good by driving yourself to sickness."

Edith sighed, and nodded her agreement to Gerd's words,
rose and retired wearily to her chamber. Thrya brought a tray

and a posset of warmed wine, but Edith was so exhausted she could not finish it. She lay down in all her clothes and sank into deep slumber. Her men kept close watch as their lady slept. It was a long night and when the sun finally rose, eyes were red-rimmed but still wakeful on the walls of Tierand.

Edith had difficulty waking the next morning. Her lids felt gritty and sore and she felt she could not face the food Thrya brought her, only drinking a cup of warm milk before hurriedly dressing in one of her older gowns.

As she joined Gerd at their usual position on the walls, she noticed immediately the air of strain and anxiety about his heavy features. Glancing along the wall at her troops she saw that they too were staring silently out towards Saer's encampment. Following their gaze, she put up her hand to shade her eyes, and for a few moments was puzzled as to what was causing the concern. Then she saw them. During the night Saer had brought his baggage wains to the front of his lines, and piled them with brushwood and other combustible items. His men had turned the carts around and, as Edith watched, started to push them slowly but inexorably towards the walls of Tierand.

As the heavy wagons approached, Edith's archers tried in vain to pick off Saer's men, but the carts gave them more than adequate cover and it was only as they came to the edge of the ditch and started to set the carts alight, that Edith's men were able to inflict some casualties on the enemy. As the brush in the carts caught fire, and thick smoke started to billow into the air, the defenders found that not only was it difficult to see the enemy because of the thick smoke, but also their eyes and noses started to sting and stream with water, blinding them most effectively and making it impossible to aim their bows into the hostile ranks of men.

Gerd dragged Edith away from the walls as the flaming carts were sent over the edge of the ditch to form a wall of fire around the keep. He snatched up a cloth, and dipping it into a vessel of fresh water, tied it over his nose and mouth. Shouting to his men to follow his example, he then upended the vessel and poured the water over himself, thoroughly soaking his hair and clothes, then he dashed up onto the walls of the keep once more, bidding Edith stay in the courtyard.

The smoke was now so thick, Edith could barely make out what was going on and it was only a resounding crash from the gates which made her realise that the enemy had finally managed to breach the doors and cut through the ropes of the drawbridge, sending it crashing down for Saer's men to pour over and into Tierand keep.

As she struggled to rub the smoke from her eyes, the tall powerful figure of Saer de Friese loomed before her disbelieving gaze. Before she could call out to Gerd for aid, Saer lunged towards her and his gauntleted fist crashed into her face opening her cheek from eye to lip in a great, bloody gash.

"That for your defiance and your insults you Saxon bitch," he snarled, then wrapping his hand in her hair he dragged her, struggling, up out of the dust and towards the doors of the hall. The whole of Tierand keep was a seething mass of fighting men, and even the women were hacking at the attackers with anything they could lay their hands on.

There was a bellow of rage as Gerd caught sight of his lady's bloodied face, and Saer's hand agonisingly tight in her hair, then the fighting intensified as fury gave added strength to her own men.

Saer hauled Edith in front of him and resting his great sword over her shoulder against her throat, screamed into her ear.

"Call off your men. Order their surrender or I'll take your head from your shoulders."

Gathering what strength she had left Edith pursed her lips and spat a bloody globule of saliva into Saer's hand.

With an oath Saer pulled back the threatening sword, but a fresh commotion without the gates made him pause and look up.

"A large force, my lord, are upon us; we have no time to secure the hold. We must flee."

With another curse Saer fought his way across the yard, hauling Edith with him, in spite of her resistance. By now, however, the pain in Edith's face was well nigh unbearable and as Saer heaved her across the withers of his horse, she passed out.

Saer leapt to the saddle and applying his spurs thundered out and over the drawbridge with his knights behind him, just as the relieving force from Runesay arrived, dust covered, and vengeful. The leader of Lord Ralf's men looked up to see the stricken figure of Gerd, slumped against the doorpost, tears pouring unchecked down his blood-spattered face, as he screamed; "That whoreson bastard's taken my lady. Get after him. Get after him." Then his sword fell from nerveless fingers and he dropped to his knees and forward onto his face. Lord Ralf's men threw themselves from their horses and rushed forward to lift Gerd and carry him into the hall. They laid him down on a pallet and Thrya, her own face sporting a livid bruise, dipped cloths in a basin of water with steeped herbs to apply to his wounds. As she attended to Gerd she tumbled forth the tale of Lady Edith's abduction and gross mis-treatment. The leader of the men from Runesay, Sir Roger, swore mightily, and quickly gave orders for men to follow after Saer and his captive.

A further challenge from the gate sent the troops diving once more for weapons, but the new arrivals proved to be none other than Arnaud and his men, on exhausted, sweat-lathered horses. He was quickly and urgently told of the situation and despite his weariness, he immediately shouted for fresh horses and was soon on the trail of his lady and her captor.

Gerd by now had recovered his senses and in spite of efforts to hold him down was roaring to chase after the Lady Edith.

It was only as Sir Roger assured him that Arnaud had arrived and was combing the area for Edith and her captors, that Gerd quieted.

The cleaning up operations began behind the walls of Tierand and it was nightfall before Arnaud and his men returned empty-handed and dispirited from the search for Edith. She and her captors had vanished almost into thin air. Hot food and ale were provided for the troops, although no-one had much of an appetite after the disastrous happenings of the day.

"My lord is following as soon as possible, but it will be a week before he arrives. We must endeavour to find the Lady Edith before that time or we are all dead men." stated Arnaud, grimly.

"The fault lies all with me, I should have watched more closely. I was careless," groaned Gerd abjectly, dropping his face in his hands in despair.

"I suggest we all get some rest," said Sir Roger, "We can do nothing tonight, and the more rested we are tomorrow, the easier we will find the search for the lady."

All nodded agreement but there were only a few who slept in fact that night beneath the roof of Tierand hold.

Edith recovered consciousness to find her hands bound tightly and cruelly behind her back. She lay on her side in a dark and stinking hovel. As she struggled to raise herself from the floor, merciless fingers fastened themselves once more in her hair, making her cry out in spite of herself as her already sore scalp was pulled painfully.

"Well well. So the Saxon bitch has come to. Let see what sort of a woman our cousin has acquired to warm his bed." With a wrench at the neck of Edith's gown Saer ripped open her bodice to the waist. Edith screamed with fury and lashed out with her feet, catching Saer full on the shins with her boots. Howling with pain, Saer gave gave her a blow which sent her crashing into the corner of the hut, opening once more the wound in her cheek and dabbling her white breasts with blood.

Saer moved towards her, then checked in mid-stride and a calculating glint came to his eye. "No, I shall not kill you now for I am sure the Lord du Fourmeils thinks highly of his comely wife. Perhaps he has even been fool enough to lose his heart to your soft white skin and cow-like gaze. I wonder what he would give to get you back in one piece?"

"Nothing," spat Edith with difficulty through swollen lips, "I am nothing to him but a means to curry favour with William.

If I die he will shrug and find another Saxon maid to bind her menfolk to William's cause."

"Think you so?" muttered Saer, almost to himself. "We shall see, we shall see." Then pulling out his knife he advanced on Edith with a cruel glitter in his eyes.

In spite of herself she shrank back, and with a gloating laugh he took a glossy brown tress in his hand and cut the lock of hair from her head.

As he left the hut, Edith sank back in despair. She must not be used as a tool in some plot of Saer's to discredit Michel or bring him harm. Edith did not really think that Saer could force Michel to give up Tierand in order to get his wife back. Did her husband care that much for her? No. Edith believed that Michel would not give up one blade of grass for her release from Saer. Therefore she must shift for herself. First of all she needed food and drink and a weapon. She must have a weapon of some kind or she stood no chance at all.

The pain in head and her face made it difficult for her to think clearly but her determination was strong. She would bide her time and let Saer think that she was cowed into submission. It would not be easy. Edith closed her eyes and fought off the wave of despair that threatened to engulf her, then her lids flew open as Saer returned through the entrance of the hovel, smiling now and looking extremely pleased with himself.

Humming a little tune he poured water into a cup and bending down to Edith he placed an arm about her shoulders and held the cup to her lips for her to drink. Edith gulped thirstily, some of the water spilling down her chin and mingling with the blood to run down between her breasts to her waist. Saer put down the cup and ran his fingers down her throat and over her breasts, smearing the blood and water in a pattern on her white skin. Edith stiffened involuntarily and Saer gave a high-pitched giggle.

"Oh you are quite safe with me my lady,"he chortled, "My tastes do not run to females you see." And as Edith's shocked gaze met his, he giggled once more and left her alone to ponder over his words.

As soon as he had left, she started to work on the ropes binding her wrists. Agonising fire burned the bruised flesh as she twisted and turned but the ropes were very tightly and expertly tied. Glancing around desperately, Edith sought something sharp on which she could scrape the ropes but a sound at the door made her look up to see one of Saer's knights step into the hut. Saying not a word, he moved towards her, and gripping her by the shoulders, raised her from the ground. He frowned at her bared breasts, then unfastening his cloak, carefully draped it over her shoulders and across her chest.

She murmured her thanks but he ignored her, simply leading her through the doorway and out into the chill air.

Saer and his men were already mounted, and her escort pushed her towards one of the mounted men, then grasping her around the waist lifted her to sit in front of him. He then mounted his own horse and Saer gave the order to move off.

They rode for several hours, until Edith was almost weeping with pain and fatigue. The feeling had long since left her bound hands and all the pain seemed to be concentrated in the ugly gash in her cheek. No-one spoke a word as the troop jingled through the forest then suddenly Saer held up his hand and his men pulled their horses to a halt. Edith peered anxiously ahead and could just make out the shape of what appeared to be a small lodge such as some of the Saxon lords had taken to building for the occasions when they were away hunting for several days.

This was obviously Saer's destination, for he looked very pleased with himself as he gave the signal to move forward once more.

When they finally halted at the door of the lodge, it was the same silent knight who came to lift Edith down. She almost fell as her feet touched the ground, but the knight supported her until she could stand, and Saer watching closely gave his high-pitched laugh.

"Erik will be your nursemaid Lady Edith. He has many talents but I personally think that his inability to speak is perhaps the most useful at times. I should not bother trying to appeal to his sympathy. He has a hatred for women which far exceeds my own. You see it was a lady friend who caused his tongue to be removed from his head."

As Saer giggled again Edith fought down the shock and nausea his words had aroused, and through her own pain and fear conveyed her sympathy to the silent knight with her eyes.

He returned her look without expression, simply turning her around and gesturing towards the lodge entrance. Stumbling slightly, Edith made her slow way into the building behind Saer and the rest of his men.

It was obvious that the lodge had been unoccupied for some time and Edith was shivering now from cold as well as fear. Erik's hand on her shoulder guided her towards a curtained off alcove containing a rough pallet bed covered with a few mangy furs and a soiled blanket. The cloak was moved aside for a moment and a knife sawed through the bonds at her wrists. Her arms fell forward and as the circulation returned to her hands, she cried out involuntarily with the agonising pain. Rough hands grasped hers and although she tried to pull them away, Erik continued to chafe them between his until finally the pain eased and she could move her fingers once more of her own accord.

She turned to Erik to thank him, but the sombre blue gaze avoided hers and the knight pushed aside the curtain over the entrance and left Edith once more alone.

Edith raised her hand and lightly explored the gash on her cheek, gritting her teeth against the pain. She could feel the encrusted blood and dirt around her eye and down to the corner of her mouth, and knew that the cut was deep and would not heal properly without leaving a scar. Misery engulfed her. Even if by some slim chance she should return to her lord, he would now turn from her in disgust at her disfigurement. True, she had been no beauty before, but now...

The swish of the curtain behind her made her turn with a

start to see Erik carrying a basin of water and some rags. Placing them on the floor he went out again to return a few seconds later with bread and meat on a platter and a cup of rough ale, putting them down beside the basin. Folding his arms, he leaned his shoulder against the door jamb and regarded Edith expressionlessly.

Uncertainly she looked from him to the food and then as he made no move, she picked up the platter and started to eat hungrily, washing down the food with the ale.

Sir Erik's unblinking stare was making her nervous and when she had finished eating, she raised her hand self-consciously to her wounded cheek. His eyes moved from her to rest on the basin of water, then he pushed himself away from the doorpost and bent to pick up the rags he had brought with him. He stood over her for a moment, then went down on one knee beside her, dipping the rags in the basin of water then squeezing out the excess.

Almost tenderly then he soaked away the dirt and blood from her face, laying bare the ugly wound Saer had inflicted. There was no salve, nor were there any herbs to ease her pain, but she made no sound or movement of protest at his ministrations, and as he finished his attentions a glint of some barely discernible emotion showed in his eyes before he turned abruptly and left the room.

Edith sat alone and waited, expecting Saer to come once more and gloat over his prisoner, but no footsteps approached her alcove and soon exhaustion made her turn to the pallet. Discarding the filthy blanket, she arranged the furs and Sir Erik's cloak into a bed. Lying down and wrapping herself into a warm cocoon Edith soon sank into a deep slumber, in spite of the pain in her face.

She was unaware of the silent shadow which loomed over her, and seeing her asleep, settled itself comfortably against the door to watch through the night, blue eyes fixed on some past scene which brought an expresion of deep hatred to his face.

13

Tierand keep was almost deserted. The gates were closed and the drawbridge was up. A scant dozen guards manned the walls searching the surrounding countryside with anxious eyes as they paced their way around the palisade. The damage caused by Saer de Friese and his men had quickly and effectively been repaired and no-one would know that the enemy had been within the gates. ...Except for the absence of the lady.

Suddenly one of the guards stiffened, and as he shaded his eyes to look towards the woods, he shouted a warning, then ducked as an arrow whistled over his head to thud into the hall behind him. His companions rushed to his side but there was no further sign of attack and they relaxed, but slowly. One of the serjeants went to pull the arrow from the wood, and as he did so, gave a curse; wrapped securely around the shaft of the arrow was a gleaming tress of hair.

Almost tumbling over in his haste, the serjerant sped down the steps and into the hall. Gerd looked up from his chair by the fire as the man entered abruptly and the words died in his throat as he saw the arrow and its decoration. He snatched the arrow from the serjeant's hand, breaking it in two with the force of his grip, then he cursed and raged as he realised what he held. However there was nothing he could do. Sir Roger, and the men from Runesay, and Arnaud with every available man from Tierand were out searching for the Lady Edith. For three days they had fruitlessly combed the surrounding countryside, leaving at dawn every morning and not returning until it was too dark to see their way any longer. They had found no trace of Lady Edith or her captors and they were beginning to despair of ever finding her...alive at least. A messenger had been sent to Runesay to inform Lady Mathild, and Edwina of their sister's fate and great had been their grief. However, it was impossible for Mathild or Edwina to leave the keep in the absence of Lord Ralf, also there was no purpose to be served by the other ladies risking their persons in a fruitless visit to Tierand.

Thrya was heartbroken! Every day saw her keeping a lonely vigil on the walls from the moment the search parties went out until long after they returned. She found consolation only in attending to the wounded Gerd. The two were fast developing a close relationship, although Gerd was much older than Thrya and had in fact been married before. He had lost his entire family in an attack on his village in Normandy by a stray band of Vikings.

That evening Sir Roger, Arnaud and Gerd sat together to discuss the arrival of the arrow with the hair attached.

"We cannot know whether this means that the Lady is alive and Saer intends to use her as a hostage against Lord Michel. Or whether Lady Edith is dead and this is Saer's cruel way of letting us know. Who can tell if further arrows may not arrive with a little more of the lady attached to them each day."

A movement of protest from Gerd and Arnaud made Sir Roger regret his grisly words, but he continued; "I have known of much worse deeds in Normandy, but I believe the Lady Edith is of more value to Saer alive than dead."

Gerd nodded at this. "That is true. He must know that if he kills her, we will hunt him down, if it means following him to hell and back."

"Yes," agreed Arnaud, "The Lady Edith is much more valuable as a hostage. I think this arrow was a preliminary to the negotiations. We have only to wait to find out what he wants, Furthermore, it is now imperative that we inform the Lord Michel of the disaster. We stand no chance of getting the lady back before he arrives home as we had hoped."

The next morning, therefore, saw three men on the road to London, each carrying a separate message in case of accidents, to inform Michel of the disaster. As it was, they met him halfway. They were unprepared for the effect of their news. Michel seemed stunned for several moments after reading what Sir Roger had written, then he passed the letter to Lord Ralf to read, staring blankly ahead as he waited. A string of curses from Ralf seemed to waken him and he turned cold, deadly eyes on the messengers. "And where were my men at this time, to allow such a thing to happen?" His voice was low but carried such venom and threat that the messengers paled to a man.

"Lord, the serjeant Arnaud had not reached Tierand at the time of the attack and the serjeant Gerd was sorely wounded trying to protect his lady," stammered the messenger whose paper Michel had read.

Michel's face flushed and his hands gripped the reins of his horse so tightly that the animal reared and screamed its protest. As its hooves hit the ground Michel jabbed it with his spurs, sending it hurtling forward almost mowing down the messengers, and leaving Ralf and his men to recover themselves and gallop after him.

It was only when his horse fell to its knees beneath him that Michel was forced to stop. He stared, panting at the foundering animal then throwing his hands up to his face, he knelt in the mud and cursed. He had to curse or he would have wept. His Edith in the hands of that perverted swine. God knows what he may have done to her.

The very thought pulled him up...Yes! By God! The Saxon lady was his. And he was not about to let her go. Nor lose her to some man-loving whoreson not fit to lick her boots.

Michel had forgotten the fact that his holding had almost been taken by de Friese. His every sense was filled with the need to recover his lady and to have revenge on his enemy, the man who had taken her.

The arrival of Ralf and the company of soldiers made him look up, then he climbed slowly and painfully to his feet. Moving to his horse he pulled the heaving animal up, and stripping his gear from it, he began to rub it down.

Lord Ralf stared at him, then made a movement towards him, but seeing the expression on Michel's face, he thought better of it. He turned away gesturing to the men to pitch camp. The men moved about silently, glancing towards Michel now and again as he continued to rub down his exhausted war horse. Finally, when hot food was ready, Ralf walked over to his friend and touched his arm. The two lords moved towards the fire and sat down, Michel staring broodingly into the flames as he toyed with the food on his plate.

"We will find your lady, never fear Michel. There are only a few places in the area where Saer could have hidden her and we shall put the full complement of our men out to search."

Michel made no reply, and while the rest of the company slept that night, he sat wrapped in his cloak staring into the flames, remembering Edith's smile and her slim body pressed to his in passion. Her soft skin and scented hair all now at the mercy of Saer's evil attentions. The Norman watched the fire through the night and they were away at dawn the next day, stopping only to rest their beasts and to wolf down some food.

When the roof of Tierand Hall came into view, Michel pulled his horse to a walk and it was at this pace that he entered the courtyard of his home. His men stood silent, unable to meet his eyes as he dismounted from his horse and climbed the steps to the hall. Gerd and Arnaud were waiting at the door and he flicked his fingers at them to follow him as he entered.

Flinging himself into his chair he shouted for food and ale then turned his gaze broodingly on his two serjeants. Their faces were grey with fatigue and the stubble lay thick on their chins. Sharp lines of worry and fear were etched on their faces and Gerd was white about the mouth with the pain from his wounds. As if satisfied with what he saw, Michel gave a curt nod and hoarsly bade then sit.

Lord Ralf and his knight entered and came to sit with Michel and his serjeants in a conference of war. They stared at the broken arrow with its tress of hair and Michel reached out to touch it then drew back his hand and thumped the table with his clenched fist.

"Where has that devil taken her? Is there no sign? Have you searched the area thoroughly?"

"My Lord," began Arnaud, "We have combed every tree, bush and log for miles around and ..." A commotion at the door made them look up to see Sir Roger struggling for breath as he entered the hall, a triumphant grin on his face, holding aloft a piece of amber material which made Michel turn pale as he recognised it...a small part of Lady Edith's bodice. All the men jumped to their feet overturning chairs in the rush to reach Sir Roger and hear his news.

"A serf's hut...one day's ride to the south," he gasped out. "There is a trail but it is not fresh and it heads into a thick part of the forest. We need huntsmen in our force if we are to follow."

At once there began a bustle of preparation. Food was readied. The force which had travelled so hard and fast from London stripped and heaved buckets of water over each other, refreshing cramped limbs. Hot food, wine and ale, and fresh clothes were distributed and fresh horses were brought in from pasture. Finally weapons were carefully, grimly but lovingly oiled and sharpened, giving clear evidence of the mood of the men from Tierand and Runesay. A small group of huntsmen were found from the village and provided with horses and promises of rich reward should they be successful in trailing the lady and her captors.

It was an impressive and determined force which left Tierand the next morning. Michel had wanted to leave immediately they were ready but Ralf had made him see the foolishness of this. It would be dark by the time they found the hut, and men and horses would benefit from a night's rest.

Otherwise what state would they be in to fight should they by any chance come quickly upon Saer and his men?

Gerd was once more left behind, much to his distress and disgust, although Thrya was quick to point out that at least the Lord Michel still trusted him enough to leave the keep in his hands. As it was, two hours after the company had left, another arrow thudded into the posts of the hall. This time it was not decorated with hair, but with a piece of parchment containing Saer's terms for the release of the Lady Edith.

Unfortunately Gerd could not read and it took time to find the priest from Runesay to decipher the message. By this time Michel and Ralf and the others were well on the road, and out of easy reach of the messenger from Tierand. Nevertheless Gerd sent out a man after him on the best horse left in the keep and then waited for the next move in the game.

14

Saer had left the lodge two days ago. Edith had heard him depart with much cursing and swearing. Her spirits rose once more as she considered her chances of escape. She was not so weak now as she had been. She had wolfed down every morsel of food Sir Erik had brought her during her imprisonment, and the pain in her cheek had subsided to a dull ache. Sir Erik's silent attentions, however, were the biggest problem. Edith was hardly left alone for a moment except for the necessary bodily functions and even then although she had privacy from his eyes, she could not escape his ears. Her only chance was to wait until he slept and this proved to be the most difficult part of her plan.

Her guard seemed tireless. For two nights after Saer had left, Edith had forced her aching lids to stay open as she waited, and waited in vain for Sir Erik to fall asleep. On the third night her vigilance was rewarded. Whether Sir Erik had taken too much wine at the evening meal, or whether his ceaseless watching had finally taken its toll, she knew not. His deep regular breathing as he lay on the pile of furs across the entrance to the alcove told her that now was her chance and she must take it. Edith picked up the dark cloak from her bed and wrapped it tightly around her, then as carefully and silently as she could she pulled aside the curtains and stepped over the sleeping warrior. Her heart rose into her mouth as the rhythm of his breathing altered slightly, then she relaxed again as it resumed its even cadence.

As softly as a wraith Edith glided along the corridor, hugging the walls closely until she turned a bend which brought her into view of the main room of the lodge. You could not call it a hall as everything was on a much smaller scale, but nevertheless, those men left by Saer to occupy the lodge and watch over his prisoner lay wrapped in their cloaks as near to the warmth of the fireplace as they could get. Edith must pass them to reach the doorway. The journey across the room was the most nerve-wracking Edith had ever made. Every mutter, every snort, every restless movement made her freeze, aware all the time that if Erik should awake and find her gone then all her chances were lost.

Finally, after what seemed hours but was in reality, only minutes, Edith reached the door. Her breathing laboured and uneven with the fear of discovery, she struggled to lift the bar as silently as possible. It was heavy, but desperation lent Edith the strength she needed and as the door swung open she took a breath of the cool night air with a grateful gasp. Still cautious, Edith pulled the door to behind her, and flattened herself against the outside wall of the lodge, inching her way along carefully until she reached the corner where she dropped into a crouch before stealing a glance around the edge of the building. No sign of guards.

Strange for Saer to be so careless but perhaps he thought he was safe, hidden away in the depths of the forest.

Still on her hands and knees, although hampered by the cloak and what remained of her gown, Edith crawled slowly across the few feet of open space until she reached the safety of the trees. Rising to her feet she picked up her skirts and fled with all the speed she could muster into the concealment of the heavy undergrowth. Desperately she pushed deeper and deeper into the forest, twigs and branches scratching her face and hands, and roots catching at her stumbling feet as she fled, until finally she could go no further and she bent her head, hands on her knees, listening to her own sobbing breath as she gasped for air.

Suddenly, she threw up her head and strained her ears as sounds came to her on the night breeze, then panic clutched her throat as she recognised those sounds as men's voices raised in anger and command. Saer's men had discovered her flight and she shuddered to think of her treatment should they recapture her. Their fear of Saer's reaction alone would make them cruel. Gathering her strength, therefore, she forced her tired limbs onwards. But she had grown crafty in her fear and instead of the blind flight which had left a crashing trail for all to follow, she now moved carefully and silently, taking care to break no twigs or branches as a mark for men to follow, and placing her feet so as to overturn no leaves, nor stones behind her.

The sounds of pursuit ebbed and flowed as her trail was followed and lost, and Saer's men cast about for signs of her passing. No fluttering, terror-stricken court lady this, but a Saxon daughter brought up to hunt and play in the forests around Sensgarth hold. Edith almost smiled at the Normans' blundering passage, but awareness of her own danger kept her mouth tight and her eyes determined.

There was not much they could do in the dark, and Saer's men finally called off the search. It was impossible to track by torchlight once they had lost the trail of Edith's first panic-stricken flight into the forest. They did not think a mere maid could get far before morning, on her own with no light or food or water. Besides, the many animals abounding in the area might do their job for them and there would not be much of the woman left to bring back.

When they had all retired back to the lodge to wait for dawn's light, one single solitary figure still stood, the blue gaze intent on the track Edith had left into the forest. A slight frown of anxiety passed over his brow. It had nothing to do with Saer de Friese but was caused by the sound of a wolf's howl floating on the night air, and the answering yips from what sounded a fairly large pack roaming the forest. The Lady Edith had no weapons with which to protect herself, and she would still be weak from her ordeal and in no state to evade a hungry wolf pack. Turning his back on the forest, Sir Erik returned to the lodge, ignoring and ignored by the rest of Saer's men. Entering the alcove where Edith had slept, the knight's nostrils flared to the faint whiff of lavender which still seemed to scent the air, then tightening his mouth grimly, Erik fastened on his sword and laced up his mail before leaving the room. Picking up a sack from the cooking area, he swiftly filled it with food and throwing a quiver of arrows over his shoulder, picked up a long ash bow and passed through the doorway into the night. One of the serjeants stared after him then shrugged and muttered to a companion. "Never gives up that one. I would not be in the Lady's shoes with him on my track." And giving a short, cruel laugh, the serjeant lay down once more to wait for light.

Edith had also heard the cry of the hunting wolf pack, and being well aware of her danger, had immediately cast about for a perch in a tree which would not be too difficult for her to climb.

A large, lightning blasted oak stood on the edge of a small clearing, and hitching up her skirts to tuck into her belt, Edith sought the easiest way up. It was difficult in the dark, and all her wounds and scratches were throbbing with pain and she felt the gash in her cheek start to bleed afresh as she finally settled herself in the rough embrace of two large branches, fairly high off the ground. Leaning her head back against the trunk of the tree, Edith forced herself to relax as she wrapped Erik's cloak around her for warmth, and dabbed the edge of it against her face to staunch the bleeding. She closed her eyes and waited impatiently for daylight.

In spite of her precarious position, and the sting of her many scrapes and scratches, Edith fell into an uneasy doze, and the sun was climbing in the sky when she finally awoke fully to stretch her cramped limbs. Her stomach rumbled with hunger, telling her that it must be long past the time for food, but she ignored it. There was nothing to fill it with anyway. Lowering herself carefully to the ground, Edith brushed down her skirts and with her fingers combed the worst of the tangles and the twigs and leaves from her hair.

There was nothing she could do about her torn bodice except wrap the cloak concealingly about her, then she inclined her head to listen for the sound of running water. A stream had run close by the lodge so if she was lucky she might find where it meandered through the trees. Glancing up at the sun in the sky, she noted its position and started off in what she hoped was a northerly direction. Edith knew from Saer's conversations with his men that they had come south from Tierand. Therefore her goal was north. Even if she did not return to her lord...her hand crept up once more to touch her face gingerly...she could let him know she was no longer a captive, and therefore he need not consider her when dealing with Saer de Friese. She wondered where Michel was now and what he was doing. Her heart and body cried out for his touch and her fingers itched to stroke once more down the long muscles of his back, making him groan with pleasure.

Her mind was brought back from its longings by the splash of water nearby, and as she pushed through the concealing bushes she gave an exclamation of delight. The stream which she had spied near the lodge had its source here, bubbling out of a natural spring in the ground to form a large clear pool edged with rocks and thick undergrowth. Many of the bushes around her bore berries, some of which she knew were edible, and hastily she gathered as many as she could into a fold of her cloak.

Sitting on a convenient rock, the Lady Edith du Fourmeils crammed the berries, sweet and sour, into her mouth to fill the empty hole which was where her stomach should have been. Then as the sun warmed her body she gazed longingly at the clear pool of water. Biting her lip she listened very intently for several long minutes, then as the only sounds she heard were were those of the birds and the small animals rustling in the forest, she compressed her lips and made up her mind.

Stripping her torn, filthy clothes from her body, and pulling off her now worn and shabby boots, Edith eased herself slowly into the icy water of the pool.

She gritted her teeth against the cold of the water where it flowed from its long dark journey underground and then she ducked her head right under the surface of the pool to scrub at the long greasy tresses of her hair. She stayed in the water as long as she could stand the cold, rubbing at her skin to remove not only the dirt and sweat, but the memory of Saer and his foul mind and words, then she turned towards the bank where she had left her clothes. Edith stood in the water, stunned for a moment as she stared at the flat stone upon which she had been sitting. Two dead rabbits now lay there, an arrow transfixing each one through the body. Behind the rabbits two mailed feet were braced apart, and Edith's shocked and despairing gaze travelled upwards until she encountered the hooded blue eyes of Sir Erik. Her teeth chattered together with cold and she closed her eyes and clasped her arms across her breasts, hugging her shoulders as a wave of fury washed over her.

Fool! She should have kept going last night in spite of the wolves and her weariness. Now she must return and face the worst wolf of all, a two-legged wolf...Saer de Friese.

Sir Erik stretched out his hand to help her from the pool and after a moment's hesitation, Edith shrugged. This Norman was no stranger to the sight of her body after a week of constant attendance on her and he was probably a man-lover like Saer anyway. The blue eyes of the knight, however, were not quite so expressionless as usual as he enfolded the slim naked body of his prisoner in the warm cloak and turning away abruptly he knelt to make a fire from dry twigs and leaves which would make no smoke. Edith wondered at his caution as she dried and dressed herself, but then dismissed the thought.

There was always the chance that Michel and the searchers from Tierand and Runesay were in the area, and there was always a danger from bands of outlaws. She went back to her first thought. Would there be any searchers from Tierand? Surely her lord would make some effort to find her even if only to take revenge on Saer for the damage to his hall and his honour.

The aroma of roasting rabbit reached her nostrils, making her mouth water and emptying her mind of all save the thought of food. Hungrily she set to when the knight offered her a share of the rabbit. When she had finished it and had licked her greasy fingers, then was sucking almost contentedly on a bone she thought she glimpsed a glimmer of a smile across his normally wooden features. Hope rose within her only to be crushed down by common sense. Why should Saer's man, a man who hated women, suddenly turn against his lord and help his hostage to escape?

Edith thought of pleading with Erik, begging him to let her go, and promising him a rich reward should he help her. But no. She would not beg the enemy for her life: She was not one to plead and she doubted that her husband would pay out large sums of money on her word. No! If she could not persuade Erik, then she must kill either him or herself to prevent Saer from using her as a weapon against her husband.

The broken shafts of the arrows with which Sir Erik had killed the rabbits lay forgotten by the ashes of the fire, and as Erik turned away to gather up their belongings, Edith swiftly snatched up the arrowhead and a portion of the shaft of one of them, concealing it in the folds of her dress as Erik turned back to her.

He regarded her flushed countenance for a moment, then seemed to shrug slightly and motioned for Edith to precede him through the trees, first scattering the ashes of the fire and obliterating all trace of their small camp.

They had been travelling for some while, Edith dragging her feet reluctantly, before she noticed that in fact they were still moving to the north, away from Saer's hunting lodge. She stopped so suddenly that Erik cannoned into her and they fell to the ground, the hard mailed body of the knight almost crushing the breath from Edith's soft frame. As he pushed himself up on his hands, Edith stared up at him watching a flush mount to his cheeks as the close contact seemed to disturb his usual cool detachment. Erik heaved a sigh and put up his hand to stroke the hair from her brow, then frowned heavily as if angry with himself and leaped to his feet, dragging Edith up with him. As he would have pushed her once more ahead of him, Edith grasped his arm and cried out to him, "Sir Erik, – No! Where are you taking me? Not to Saer, the lodge lies south, please take me home." And in spite of her efforts at control, the huge tears spilled down her cheeks and she sobbed out all her pain and despair in the comforting arms of the silent knight.

Sir Erik cursed inwardly. How could he explain? Even he was confused by his feelings. How could he tell the lady of his decision to return her safely to her lord? He would probably die for his pains. If du Fourmeils did not kill him, he knew Saer would not rest until he had his revenge on the knight for betraying him. Sir Erik did not consider his oath of fealty to Saer to be binding any longer. The atrocities he had witnessed during his service to the lord absolved him from his obligations.

Edith's sobs became a whimper and finally she calmed down and wiped her face with the edge of her cloak. She said nothing, merely stood waiting for a decision from him. An awkward smile twisted his lips and he nodded and patted her hand, pushing her in the direction they had been taking. Slowly she turned, amazed at the turn of events, and the two continued through the forest to escape their pursuers.

They were doomed to failure. As they crossed a small clearing in the forest, a shout rang out and Sir Erik turned, drawing his sword and pushing Edith behind him to protect her. As she strained to see around him, despair engulfed her. Saer's men crowded triumphantly into the clearing and spread out slowly to surround them. Sir Erik hefted his sword, prepared to fight to the death for the Lady du Fourmeils.

Gerd's messenger reached Michel as the lord was about to take his force into the forest around the hovel where Sir Roger had found the torn fragment of Lady Edith's bodice.

The air was filled with curses as Michel read Saer's insulting terms for the release of his wife. Then crushing the parchment in his fist, he flung it from him as far as he could.

"The dog demands everything...everything...my lands here and in Normandy, my titles, even the very ring I wear which was my mother's. Damn him to hell. If we do not find my lady quickly, I shall lose everything I possess."

"You intend to give what he asks then, for the return of your lady?" queried Ralf, watching Michel closely.

Michel was silent for a moment staring down at the pommel of his saddle, then he raised eyes which were filled with such a mixture of misery, fury and despair that Ralf winced away and could not meet their gaze.

"What else can I do?" he whispered hoarsely, then turning away from Ralf he shouted for the huntsmen.

They crowded round him answering his questions eagerly.

"What force?"

"Not large, lord,...perhaps fifty men. Enough to leave clear tracks for eyes used to tracking game."

The leader of the group of huntsmen grinned nastily. "We have him lord. It is a track a child could follow."

98

"Then follow it!" snarled Michel, his expression making even the hardened men about him glance at each other and pale. With their harness and weapons padded to make little sound, Michel and Ralf and their men melted into the forest on the trail of Saer and his captive. The huntsmen had dismounted from their horses and left them tethered back at the hut with a small guard of men. It was the leading huntsman now, who moved ahead his eyes searching the forest trail expertly, picking out the tracks of Saer and his men. It was after several hours of silent tracking that he came moving back through the trees to Michel's stirrup, his face puzzled and wary as he gauged the lord's reaction to his news.

"Well, what is it?" hissed Michel.

"I am not sure lord. There is an old hunting lodge ahead with only four or five men occupying it. There are signs that the whole troop was quartered there but at least half moved out two or three days ago and those who are left search for something or someone to the north of here."

Michel too was puzzled. Had Saer left, taking Edith with him? Or had she managed to escape and was now being hunted through the woods like an animal? The thought brought a mixture of hope and fear to his breast. Hope that Edith had indeed escaped, and fear of what would happen to her, when or if they recaptured her before Michel and his men could reach her.

Gesturing to Ralf, Michel whispered the huntsman's news and his own conclusions. He saw similar emotions to his own chase across Ralf's features, then the two lords turned their horses' heads as one in the direction the huntsman indicated.

Sacrificing caution for speed now, the company crashed through the forest in pursuit of their quarry. Michel's lips were drawn back from his teeth in a silent snarl and the eyes were as cold and cruel as Edith had ever imagined them to be.

Their sudden arrival in a large clearing made them halt in surprise for a moment and then with a scream of rage which turned the blood cold of every man present, Michel drew his sword and jabbing in his spurs, hurtled forward.

Ralf held his men back as he took in the scene before him. The Lady Edith stood with her back to a tree, her hands clutching a cloak to her breast, her hair in wild disarray around her face. In front of her stood a solitary knight obviously sorely wounded but with a pile of four or five men, dead or dying around him and his sword bloodied thickly to the hilt. He was breathing with difficulty and leaned on his sword as the ring of Saer's men closed in on him only to halt their advance as Michel screamed his fury behind them.

They turned to face the fresh danger only to be hewn down where they stood by Michel's singing sword or his horse's heavily shod hooves. All that was left for Lord Ralf and the rest of the company to do was to cut down those who tried to escape the raging madman striking to left and right in blind fury. When there were no more men left to kill, Michel pulled his horse to a halt and sat for several moments trying to clear his brain of the red murder which had sent him berserk. The sight of Edith and the condition she was in had sent him wild and now he fought for control. The sword fell from his hand and stuck quivering in the earth. Then, as his men watched silently, he tossed his leg over the front of his saddle and slid to the ground.

He walked unsteadily towards Edith, the swaying knight still holding himself protectively in front of her as Michel's eyes never left the ugly gash on his lady's face.

As he reached where Sir Erik stubbornly stood, blue eyes stared into black for a moment before Sir Erik crumpled to the ground and Michel was taken aback at the sight of his wife falling to her knees with a cry to pull at the still form at her husband's feet. A cold mask descended over Michel's face as he reached down to jerk Edith to him. The cloak fell from her shoulders and he went white at the sight of her torn bodice and bared breasts covered in scratches and dark bruises.

Edith threw back her head and stared defiantly at her lord. Let him see how disfigured she was so that she could get his disgust and repudiation over with whilst she still had the courage to bear it. Sir Erik had died defending her and she would not see his body left for the animals to tear at.

Michel pulled the cloak to cover his lady then stooping swiftly he lifted her in his strong arms and carried her, struggling, to his horse.

She gasped out her protest, calling Sir Erik's name, then stilled as her lord spoke. "Rest easy my lady, your protector comes with us."

Edith looked over his shoulder as Lord Ralf's men wrapped Sir Erik carefully in a cloak and hastily prepared a stretcher slung between two horses in which to place him. Then Michel mounted his warhorse behind Edith and the company moved off once more into the trees.

They spent the night at the hunting lodge. What was left of Saer's men hastily retreated at the sight of Michel's force and Michel let them go, to run to Saer and tell him of the failure of his plans.

Sir Erik's wounds were tended to by Ralf's men. He was badly injured but Ralf had bound a warrior's wounds many times and although Sir Erik was still unconscious, he had no fever.

Michel spoke no word to Edith as the fires were lit and a meal made ready, but beckoned her to him, helping her to a chamber close to the alcove she had previously occupied. On trembling limbs she moved with him, glancing past the curtain to her former bed in this place. He followed her look, noting the furs spread to form a bed across the threshold. His expression lightened a little but he still did not speak until the door of the chamber closed behind him.

Michel grasped his wife's shoulders and pulled her to him staring into her eyes as though he would lay bare her soul. Edith could not meet his look. She raised her hand to cover the ugly scabs on her face but he grasped her fingers and pulled her arms behind her back, holding then easily with one hand as he searched her face and she struggled to hide her features from him.

"Who did this?" he whispered hoarsely and she answered through trembling lips; "Saer. He struck me down when he

tried to take Tierand. He did not touch me after that. He..."
Her voice tailed away as disgust rose to choke her then Michel
spoke abruptly.

"I know...Saer was never as other men. You were not in
that sort of danger from him. But the other...who is he?"

"Sir Erik, one of Saer's knights. He was my guard but after I
managed to escape he caught up with me alone, then would
not let them take me when they tracked us down. I know not
why he protected me..."

She stopped as Michel uttered a sneering laugh, then continued:

"Saer told me that a woman had caused the knight's tongue
to be ripped out and that therefore he hated all women. I think
that he hoped Sir Erik would be cruel to me, but he was not."
She ran out of words and stood, waiting for his reaction. He
grasped her shoulder, pulling her into his embrace.

"It seems your knight did not have time to take his payment
from you. Well then you can pay me instead for the days I have
spent searching for you, and the men I have killed to take you
back."

He did not know why he said the bitter words. But they
were out before he realised and then with a groan his mouth
fastened hard and demanding on hers, her bruised body
pressed punishingly against his mail. She beat ineffectively at
him as his tongue plunderd the sweetness of her mouth,
writhing in his hard embrace to escape him. It was no use. As
he used his strength on her she felt she would break in two
and her heart cried out against his treatment of her. Had she
endured days of misery and fear to suffer at the hands of her
own husband? Her frantic fingers knocked against something
caught in the folds of her skirts and she grasped at the
arrowhead without being aware of what she did.

Pulling out the weapon she had picked up only that morning, she raised it high and struck at the Norman lord she had
taken for her husband.

Fortunately he was still wearing his mail, and although the
arrow pierced the mesh links it did not penetrate very far into

his flesh. Far enough however for the pain to cut through the clouds of emotion raging in him. With a curse he flung her from him and as she fell to the floor she spat at him through the curtain of her hair.

"So, my lord, I have escaped rape and degradation at the hands of my captors, only to meet it from my own husband."

He stared at her in agony for a moment then without further sign or sound he turned and left the room, slamming the door behind him.

Edith took a deep, shuddering breath, then pushed herself up from the floor with her hands. The arrowhead lay by the bed, his blood staining the point and she bent to pick it up and stare at it for several seconds before throwing the weapon from her with sudden repugnance. Oh God! It was a wonder he did not have her killed. It was his right to take her, whenever and however he wished. It was just... he had been so tender before, she could not allow him to take her like a whore. How could he believe that she had sold herself in order the achieve her escape.

Suddenly it was all too much for her and tremors shook her body as she sobbed out her anguish and grief, falling onto the bed to hide her face in the furs.

Michel's emotions too were in a turmoil. The scratch from the arrow head was nothing... he had received worse cuts scraping the hair from his face. It was the way he had just treated his own wife! How could he have abused her when she had gone through so much? It was jealousy which made him so cruel. And she... she had struck at him with all her strength. If he had not been wearing his mail it would have been much worse. A sudden glow of pride startled him. How could he believe that his Saxon falcon would lay with another man merely to gain her freedom.

But now what should he do? Should he try and win her afresh? Or should he let her go?

The thought of her warm slim body in his arms and her breasts pushing against the muscles in his chest made him groan and his body responded to the thought with a force which made him doubt his ability to send Edith from him. He shook his head. These thoughts would drive him insane. He would take some ale with Ralf and the men, and try to drown his urges for a while.

When he finally stumbled back to the bedchamber, somewhat the worse for drink, Edith had fallen into an exhausted slumber and did not wake as he entered the room. He gazed blearily down at her swollen features for a short moment, then passing his hands wearily over his face, the strain of the past weeks took its toll and he lay down beside his wife and sank into sweet oblivion.

16

The following morning Edith awoke before her lord, and after gazing at him beside her for a moment, she rose from the bed and went to search for water to wash with and to bathe her cuts and bruises and her swollen eyes.

She met Lord Ralf on her way through the hall and his shocked sympathetic eyes made her want to burst into tears again. However, she merely gave him a strained smile and moved to pass him. He took her arm as she passed and as she looked enquiringly, he murmured, "You must make allowances for Michel. He has been under severe strain these days gone by. Saer's demands were heavy but he thought he would lose you if he did not agree to them. He..."

"Ralf!" Michel's voice cracked out like a whiplash, effectively silencing Ralf and sending Edith spinning round, her eyes full of questions. Michel stood leaning against the entrance of the corridor and his eyes held a warning. Whether it was for Ralf or herself Edith did not know but she inclined her head, avoiding his look and hurried away.

Filling a basin with water, Edith washed her hands, bathing the cuts on her arms, then splashing the water onto her face carefully avoiding the healing tissue on her cheek with her fingers. She reached out for a cloth to dry herself, and tensed as a strong brown hand reached out to pass it to her. She dabbed the water carefully from her face, then winced away as he captured her chin and turned her cheek to the light.

She glared at him defiantly, and a faint smile twisted his lips as he murmured, "And so Madame, you are marked for me. I shall exact full payment never fear." Then he turned from her and went out, and she heard him shouting to his men to make ready for the journey home.

When Edith left the lodge and searched for her mount, there was none for her until her lord turned his horse towards her and leaned down to lift her before him, still muffled in Sir Erik's cloak. Her eyes slid to the stretcher which still carried the injured knight.

"We shall take him home with us and care for him with the rest of our men." Michel murmured in her ear.

"My thanks lord," replied Edith stiffly. He sighed at her tone, but she did not understand his attitude this morning. Was he still drunk?

No! His eyes were clear and his speech distinct. The contempt was gone from his face, and his arms held her closely to him.

All of a sudden Edith felt much better, in spite of her wounds and her exhaustion and bedraggled appearance.

Their progress through the forest now was slow, the strain of the past two weeks showing on all their faces. Michel and Lord Ralf and those men who had accompanied them to London had not stopped to rest in all that time, and both the lords were thinner, with lines of weariness in their faces.

Lord Ralf rode next to Michel.

"What about Saer now? We don't know where he is or what he may be up to."

An expression of such hatred and cruelty came over Michel's face, that Edith recoiled. His arms tightened around her.

"Wherever he is and whatever he may be doing, I shall find him. And when I do, he will wish he had never been born."

Lord Ralf placed his hand on Michel's arm.

"You must be careful. You hold your lands now of William and cannot afford to upset him. You must be as crafty as Saer and make a formal complaint, challenging him to meet you body to body."

"No!" gasped Edith, then coloured as both lords turned their eyes on her incredulously. It was not a woman's place to question her lord.

"Fear not my lady, I would ensure that you would be provided for should Saer be the victor. You would not have to deal with such as him again."

Edith wanted to cry out that she did not care what happened to her if he should be killed, but she could not. Even if Ralf had not been there she could not bear the disbelief and cynicism in her husband's eyes. One thing she vowed. If Saer was to kill Michel then one way or another she would make sure that the Norman man-lover did not survive him long enough to enjoy the fruits of his victory.

They stopped at the hut where Saer had first kept Edith, and picked up the horses for the huntsmen and the few men they had left on guard. Although there were now spare horses, Michel did not relinquish his wife to allow her to ride on her own, but kept her in front of him, his arms securely about her.

Night had fallen by the time the company had reached Tierand keep and as they made their slow and weary way towards the familiar walls, torches flared on the palisade and the guards shouted the challenge. At Michel's reply the drawbridge came rattling down and the gates opened to reveal all those who had been left behind now tumbling into the yard in various states of disarray to greet their lord and make anxious enquiries about the Lady Edith.

At sight of Edith carried in Michel's arms, shouts of triumph went up and Gerd and Thrya pushed their way through the crowding soldiers to help her down and into the hall.

Lord Michel, however, leaped from his horse, and threw the reins to a groom with shouted instructions to feed the beast well. He caught up with them at the top of the steps, and lifting Edith once more in his arms, carried her to their chamber.

A fire was burning in the hearth and in the peace and quiet of the room it was difficult to believe that the events of the past two weeks had really happened.

Gently removing Edith's cloak, Michel turned her around to help her take off her ruined gunna. A knock at the door heralded Thrya's arrival with two servants carrying the tub and buckets of hot water.

"I know it is late my lady, but I thought you would wish to bathe before lying once more in your own bed."

"Oh Thrya, that would be wonderful," sighed Edith. Thrya turned to Michel with a bob of her head.

"Ranulf your squire has prepared a bath for you in the next chamber my lord if it please you."

It did not really please Michel at all to leave Edith at this point, but the thought of a hot bath was very tempting, and he would return afterwards. So after one more lingering glance towards Edith, Michel left the room.

As soon as he had departed, the two Saxon women were in each other's arms, laughing and crying at the same time.

"Oh my lady, your poor face. That swine has hurt you cruelly. Let me attend to your wounds."

Thrya helped Edith into the bath and after carefully washing her mistress's hair, she turned attentions to the wound on her face. Soaking the scabs with hot water, Thrya peeled them away.

There was very little bleeding which showed that it was healing well.

Thrya gently washed Edith's face with a soft cloth, avoiding the wound and after drying it she applied some healing ointment which would lubricate the skin and lessen the pull on the new tissue forming underneath.

Edith rose from her bath feeling much better and walked over to a small table where some food had been set for her and her lord. While Thrya saw to the removal of the tub, and went down to fetch some hot spiced wine, Edith ate hungrily, wondering when Michel would return. Surely he had finished bathing by now?

Michel had indeed finished bathing, and Ranulf his squire, was attending to his wounds. He frowned when he came across the arrow wound on Michel's shoulder which Edith had inflicted.

"You did not say you were wounded yesterday, lord, I saw no archers."

"'Tis nothing. A mere pinprick. The result of carelessness," he answered, with a humourless grin.

Carelessness indeed! He had been careless with his lady falcon after all her trials, and she had meted out fitting punishment.

He brooded on what he should do next. She would not want to lie with him this night after all she had been through. Best to stay away from her until she forgot her attachment to Saer's knight. If he went to her chamber now, he would take her there and then, willing or not, weary or not.

"Arrange a bed in here for me tonight Ranulf. I do not wish to disturb my lady after all she has endured and I am sore weary myself."

Ranulf stared for a moment, then shrugged. A considerate lord this, not wanting to impose himself on an exhausted woman.

Ranulf went out to fetch food and wine for Michel and to collect furs for the narrow bed in his chamber.

When the bed was ready, Michel stretched his weary limbs upon it, but it was some time before his eyelids closed in sleep, his body aware of Edith just next door, and wanting her with every fibre of his being.

Edith too lay sleepless. Ranulf had knocked with the message that her lord would not disturb her tonight and she had almost cried out with the pain of rejection. She had not yet looked in her mirror to assess the damage to her face, but she had not noticed anyone turning from her in revulsion. Therefore it could not be so bad.

Perhaps he still thought her a whore.

Perhaps he would not come to her bed ever again!

But that was nonsense! he must come to her even if only to

beget his heirs on her body. He would not have fought so hardily for his holding simply to let it go with his death. No, he must come to her some time, and when he did she would be warm and willing.

She knew she could not live without him. And on this decision Edith finally fell asleep.

The next morning saw the departure of Lord Ralf and his men. He bid them farewell with an anxious frown on his face. Something was very wrong between these two and he was not sure how he could help them. Perhaps his lady would know what to do. His face cleared and his eyes brightened at the thought of seeing Mathild again after so long away. He finished his farewells somewhat hastily, and rode speedily through the gates of Tierand, his eyes fixed ahead and his face alight with anticipation.

Edith watched his departure with a twinge of envy which she quickly banished. She wished her sister all the joy in the world, but could not help feeling a little bitter at her own lord's attitude.

He had scarcely spoken to her that morning and he avoided her for the rest of the day. He was silent at mealtimes, and flinched from the contact each time his hand met hers. Edith was in despair. She knew not what she should do, or how to react to him.

Finally she decided on an air of calm dignity. Not too cool, but polite and pleasant. Oddly enough this seemed to make the situation worse. Michel cast her glowering looks and when he did speak to her he almost snarled.

She had been to visit Sir Erik who had recovered consciousness and seemed to be mending well. His blue eyes were still
distant but he managed a smile when he saw her.

Michel fumed at her side during the visit then strode back to
the hall at such a pace that Edith could not keep up with
him. Even Thrya noticed his mood and cast sympathetic eyes
towards her mistress.

A messenger had been sent off to William with a formal
complaint against Saer de Friese, and a demand for satisfaction
and justice from the King. They had only to await a reply now,
and Michel concentrated on getting himself fit and on readying
his weapons and his warhorse for the combat which he was
sure would be arranged.

Edith hid her anxiety so well that Michel became even more
convinced that she did not care whether he lived or died in the
challenge, only in so far as it affected herself. He spoke to her
of this at the evening meal.

"My lady you need not concern yourself over your fate
should I fail in combat with de Friese. I have arranged with
Lord Ralf that you are to go to him at Runesay should the
worst befall, and I have left with him a large sum of money for
your needs."

Edith stared at him open-mouthed for a moment, then anger
lent strength to her voice as she replied.

"You mistake my mettle, my lord if you think that I would
require anything after your death. I can take care of myself
should your cause fail at William's court."

Bleakness settled over his features and his voice was cold.

"Madame, you will not bring dishonour on my house or my
name. You will do as I say. You have no choice."

"Why you arrogant oaf," she blazed, "I hope you go down
without a chance beneath the man-lover. I would not pray for
your soul if you left me all your fortune after your death."

Tipping over her chair, Edith picked up her skirts and fled
up the stairs to her chamber. After a moment of blank in-
credulity, Michel became aware of the stares of his men and
clearing his throat, excused himself before following his wife

with black murder in his heart.

Edith had locked her chamber door behind her, but that did not stop her furious lord. Putting his shoulder to the latch he applied his considerable strength to opening it and it flew back with a crash.

She retreated before him and he kicked the door to as he advanced on her, all thoughts of restraint and kindness flown from his mind as he seethed over her words.

'Arrogant oaf' she had called him, and tossed his concern back in his face. Very well, he may as well take from her what he could, while he could. There was always the chance that Saer would defeat him in the battle and then they would be shovelling the cold soil onto his face.

Edith was shaking with fear. Would he kill her now? Her words had been unpardonable but they had flown from her tongue before she could stop them. She did not really wish him dead. She wanted him warm and strong and alive...and in her bed, God forgive her.

At that moment the backs of her knees met the bed behind her and she toppled backwards, unable to save herself. As she rolled to get up, the Norman flung himself across the room and atop her struggling body.

In his twenty-odd years Michel had been no stranger to sub- duing unwilling women, and he used his weight now to hold her down, one leg flung across her thighs, and his hand hold- ing both of hers stretched high above her head.

"So madame, you think to rid yourself of me so that you can choose a lover more to your taste? Well, I may as well have my money's worth if I am to fight for you again. Perhaps if I leave you breeding you will be less willing to look for another." And his mouth crashed onto hers, his tongue demanding entry to her sweetness.

Conflicting emotions fought within Edith's brain. Her mind rejected his words and his attitude but her body cried out treacherously for his. The melting fire of desire swept through her limbs leaving her trembling and breathless. Her throat ached with her love for him and she tried to convey capitulation with her body.

Michel sensed her surrender and his lips softened their cruel attack, allowing her mouth to open and her tongue to meet his in sweet response. He let go of her hands and her arms crept up and around his neck, her fingers lovingly caressing the burnished curls at his nape. He groaned, and raised himself to stare at her. She immediately turned her face to one side, attempting to conceal the ugly scar but he would have none of this, and taking her chin in his strong fingers so that she could not shrink from him, he laid his lips to the ridge of scar tissue.

"You belong to me little falcon. You are marked for me and no other shall have you."

Edith stiffened at his words. He did not speak of love. He never had, but Edith was prepared to accept his desire for her and as he slowly undressed her she tried to blank out all thoughts of what she would do should he be taken from her in the forthcoming battle.

Her breath caught in her throat as his naked body blocked out the light above her and she gave a small cry as she caught sight of the wound in his shoulder which she had inflicted with her arrow. Then a smile curved her lips.

"Well my lord, if I am marked for you, then you will also be marked for me."

His reply was to silence her very effectively by kissing her.

The flames flared high between them, but Michel was in no hurry. He was determined to savour this night with his Saxon falcon, and allow no haste to spoil their pleasure.

His mouth explored her skin, bringing small whimpers of delight from her as her nerves thrilled to his touch. He held his weight off her as he experimented where he had not before, subduing her protests with his teeth and tongue. Edith was quick to learn, and she retaliated with caressing fingers until he could stand no more and plunged to his pleasure, his lady meeting him halfway with sighs of ecstasy. Michel spoke no word afterwards, simply pressed his lips to hers before relaxing at her side into a deep slumber. Edith's thoughts kept her awake for some time, but finally her body succumbed to her weariness and she too slept.

Her dreams troubled her and when she awoke with a cry in the early hours of the morning it was to find the bed empty beside her. A sense of desolation assailed her. He had slipped away with no word or farewell caress. If he could leave her so easily after their lovemaking it surely showed that he did not care for her except as a body to satisfy his lust.

She bent her knees up under the covers, resting her chin upon them with a sigh. She felt stifled. She must get away from him for a short while even though she knew she would miss the sight and sound and feel of him. But where could she go? Not to Mathild; her sister was too sharp-eyed and Edith did not feel like answering a barrage of questions just now. She would go home to her father's holding. The more she thought about it, the more the idea pleased her. Michel could have no objection. It would be surly of him to refuse to allow her to visit her parents, especially after the ordeal she had just been through. Giving a nod of satisfaction, Edith tossed back her hair and called for Thrya to help her wash and dress. The maid came through the door rubbing her hands over her eyes and straightening her dress. Edith ignored her reproachful looks over the early hour and briskly ordered some food and milk to break her fast.

Once dressed she steeled herself to face her lord with her request.

Michel was in the courtyard watching Ranulf trot his destrier up and down, a concerned frown on his face over the animal's slight lameness.

Edith stood patiently to one side until he should have finished and could give her his attention. He glanced at her from beneath his lashes and that simple action sent her heart racing. 'Oh God, how can I leave him? Even should he treat me as the dirt beneath his feet, at least I could see and touch and hear him.' Then she stiffened her resolve. Better to get away and allow herself some time to order her emotions and control the treacherous leap of her heart at the mere sight of him.

He finally turned to her after signalling that Ranulf should put the horse away and send for the blacksmith to check his feet.

"Yes my lady?" he questioned, his expression polite as he took her arm.

"My lord, I have a favour to ask, if you could but spare me a few moments to listen."

"Another one?" he paused a moment his eyes fastened to hers as she raised them beseechingly. What he saw there made him frown and turn away with an impatient shrug.

"Very well madame. Ask away."

Edith felt the familiar surge of anger at his attitude, but she fought it down and kept her voice calm as she made her request.

He did not reply at first and Edith's heart sank as he simply waved her ahead of him into the hall, then he seemed to come to a sudden decision.

"An understandable desire, lady, to visit your parents. I think that perhaps it would be better at the moment for you to be under your father's protection. I have no doubt that William will accede to my demand for satisfaction. He will have no choice as I am sure he knows more of this affair than I would like. William is a devout man and a loving husband. He will be furious that Saer allowed things to go so far."

"And will Saer reply to your challenge?"

"He also will have no choice. Besides, he will not lightly pass by the opportunity to kill me and acquire all I possess, legally."

Edith pressed her lips together at the thought.

"Do I go with you this time my lord?"

Michel regarded her searchingly before replying.

"I would prefer you to be out of Saer's reach should aught go awry," he said heavily. "Therefore go to your father's hold and remain there until I send for you, or until you hear news of the outcome of the trial of arms."

Edith felt the colour leave her cheeks, but simply bent her

head to her lord and turned away to prepare for the journey to her father's. She missed his outstretched hand and he dropped it back to his side as he watched her hurry away from him, then turning swiftly he strode out of the door to call for his horse. Within minutes he had ridden through the gates and out towards the hills.

18

The next day saw Edith on the road to Sensgarth. The weather was dry and bright and they would make better time than they had on their first journey over that road. She had with her Gerd and a company of men for her protection and they would spend their first night at Runesay to collect any messages or presents from Mathild and Edwina for their parents.

A kind of desperation had hold of Edith as she rode along in the soft clear sunlight. Michel had not come to her bed the previous night. He had stayed out all day after granting her request, returning only for the evening meal and to make arrangements for the journey. He had spoken to her only when necessary, spending most of his time staring broodingly into his wine. He had drunk far more than usual. All her attempts at conversation came to naught. She finally gave up in despair, pushing back her plate after scarcely touching her food and murmuring her wish to retire.

Her lord simply nodded his head, muttering a scant good-night as she mounted the stairs with her head held high and her back straight, fighting back the tears.

She had held onto her control until Thrya had left her, then as she lay alone in the great bed with the time passing and no sign of her lord coming to her, she allowed the sadness to over-whelm her. Eventually she had cried herself to sleep, missing the lean shadow which came to stand by the bed after making sure she slept. Regarding her swollen lids and flushed cheeks with unreadable eyes, he then turned away to cast himself on the pallet bed in the next chamber.

The Norman tossed and turned, until dawn when he finally rose and, shiveringly, doused his face and body with cold water before descending to arouse Gerd with careful instruction regarding his care of the Lady Edith. The serjeant swore grimly that no harm would come to her while there was a breath in his body, and satisfied with this Michel turned into the hall to take some food.

When Edith descended the stairs after eating in her chamber, Michel's mind was occupied with the preparations for the coming trial with Saer, and to Edith he seemed to have already forgotten her existence. As he lifted her to her horse, however, his fingers lingered at her waist, then slid caressingly down her thigh making her stomach churn and her fingers weaken on the reins of her palfrey. Feeling the lack of control, the creature danced away and Edith was forced to concentrate on keeping her seat.

When she at last looked to her lord he had turned his head to listen to Arnaud at his side and the moment was gone.

As they left Tireand Edith strained her head around over her shoulder to catch sight of Michel on the walls of the palisade. He lifted his arm in farewell, but before she could return his wave he had moved from her sight.

Michel could not bear to see her go. After a quick wave from the walls of the keep, he turned away. There was something important for him to attend to.

Sir Erik was conscious and sitting up when Michel entered, although no expression crossed his face as he watched the lord approach.

Michel came straight to the point.

"Sir Erik, as a knight you are forsworn. You have broken your oath of fealty to Saer."

Sir Erik watched him unblinkingly.

Michel turned away, choosing his next words carefully.

"I have complained to William about Saer's attack on me, and his abduction of my wife. I have issued a challenge to Saer to meet me in armed combat. If I succeed in this you will be free...free to swear to another lord."

A brief smile flickered across the knight's mouth as Michel made the point and then he nodded, just once, holding Michel's gaze with his own.

That satisfied Michel. He moved to leave the room then stopped and turned back to the pallet where Sir Erik lay.

He leaned close...

"I never thanked you. She means everything to me."

The smile this time was deeper and Sir Erik lifted a hand in denial.

Then Michel turned abruptly and left the knight to rest.

Suddenly he felt a lot better.

* * *

Edith was jerked from her musings by Gerd's hand on her arm.

"Not far now to Runesay, my lady. They will be glad to see you there safe and sound."

"Yes Gerd. I look forward to seeing my sisters again."

...'Although I hope Mathild does not ask too many question' she thought.

As it was the questions did come thick and fast but they were not the kind of questions Edith had feared. Overjoyed at her safety, Mathild and Edwina needed to assure themselves of her well-being although Mathild was puzzled at Edith leaving her husband so soon after her rescue.

Edith explained it away by saying that Michel feared for her safety should Saer defeat him at the tourney.

"Ha! Not much chance of that." bellowed Ralf. "Although Saer is a big man he is soft and not as experienced a fighter as Michel. Have no fear Lady Edith, your lord will take his revenge in full measure."

Edith was glad of Ralf's confidence in her lord and forced herself not to even consider the possibility of his defeat. Mathild exclaimed over the mark on Edith's face but was sure that it would eventually fade into only a thin scar.

Edith basked in the attention and affection she was receiving and her spirits rose as Mathild showed her around Runesay, now much cleaner and sweeter smelling than on Edith's last visit. She praised Mathild's hard work and congratulated Edwina on some tapestries her young sister had worked for the bedchambers.

It was only at the evening meal that Edith's spirits drooped once more. She pictured the lean and graceful frame of her husband in the chair now occupied by Sir Roger, and she crumbled her bread on the trencher, her throat too tight to eat.

Mathild frowned as she noticed her sister's pre-occupation but deemed it wiser to say nothing. She tried to distract Edith with her speculations on their parents' reactions to their daughter's visit.

"You must assure them that we are all most content with our lives, and stress to our father, the fairness and justice of William as King. I think it may be best if you do not tell them of the forthcoming combat. It would only worry them unnecessarily."

Edith nodded her agreement, then put up a hand to stifle a yawn. Laughingly she excused herself and Mathild suggested that they all retire early as Edith must leave at first light the next day if she were to get a good start on the journey to Stensgarth.

Surprisingly Edith slept deeply and dreamlessly and she felt refreshed and quite optimistic when she awoke the next morning.

The sun was shining again as they prepared to leave Runesay and Edith glanced up at the blue sky where a lark was carolling sweetly.

"Well it looks as if your journey will be more comfortable than when we came here," sighed Mathild as she stood to bid

farewell to Edith in the courtyard, and Edith's thought flew
back to the miserable trip they had made from Sensgarth and
the fears and uncertainties which had troubled the three Saxon
women at the time.

Gerd touched her elbow to indicate that they were ready to
leave and Edith, Mathild and Edwina embraced each other
warmly before the company from Tierand turned their horses'
heads and trotted out of the gate and away.

The trip passed smoothly and quickly and Edith felt herself
relaxing under Gerd's assiduous attentions to her comfort. His
obvious devotion and care was like a balm to her sorely bruised
heart.

The familiar outline of the hall eventually came into view
and Edith pulled up her horse for a moment to breath in the
scents and sounds of her childhood. Suddenly with an un-
ladylike whoop and callous disregard for her escort, Edith
clapped her heels to her horse's sides and galloped full tilt
towards her father's hold.

The gates stood wide and as Edith thundered through them
with her escort close behind, alarm and confusion spread
through Sensgarth bringing her father out of the hall at the
run, unsheathing his sword and throwing the scabbard away
behind him. His jaw dropped open as he realised who was on
the curvetting horse, hair falling from its demure braids and
cheeks flushed with exertion. His expression changed from
alarm to delight to anger as he roared at his daughter.

"Edith! What do you think you're doing girl, frightening us
out of our wits? You could have been killed in mistake for an
enemy."

Edith laughed down into his face.

"A fine watch you keep father. If I had been an enemy you
would all be dead or captured at this very moment."

The truth in her words made her father flush, then he looked
at the hand holding his sword and let it drop to his side with a
sheepish grimace.

"Ord!" he bawled, "Take the Lady Edith's horse and show
her men where they can stay." He moved forward to help his

daughter down from her horse but Gerd was there before him, his hands solicitous as he lifted her to the ground.

Her father quirked an eye-brow at the serjeant's care, then ushered Edith into the hall.

The Lady Beatrice, Edith's mother, was standing at the foot of the stairs, her teeth biting her bottom lip and her hands clenched into fists, the knuckles showing white.

As her anxious eyes met Edith's, the expression in their depths changed to one of incredulous joy. She opened her arms and Edith flew to their comfort and found herself clasped to her mother's warm, sweet-smelling bosom.

Laughing and crying at the same time Edith and her mother hugged and kissed each other until Lord Rufus interrupted them by clearing his throat noisily.

"My lady, if you would take Edith to her chamber to refresh herself, we can hear all her news over the meal."

Lady Beatrice threw her hands in the air and apologising for her lack of consideration for her daughter and how tired she must be, took Edith up the stairs to the familiar bedchamber. Once inside, her mother leaned her back against the wall and watched as Edith walked round the room, her fingers trailing over familiar objects and her eyes picking out the well remembered marks and stains of their life in this hall before they were swept away by the Norman lords.

Edith sighed and turned to her mother, "Everything seems smaller somehow and the colours not as bright as I remember."

Lady Beatrice smiled a little sadly, "My dove, you have grown up, that is all. Your eyes have been opened to newer, stranger things than your life here."

Her daughter flopped onto the bed which felt hard and un-yielding after her soft feather mattress at Tierand.

"Yes, you're right, mother, I am not the same person I was when I left here months ago. I feel very much older although not very much wiser," and Edith laughed at the thought of the wide-eyed, innocent maid she had been.

Lady Beatrice asked the question which had been trembling

on her tongue since she had first embraced her daughter; "And the Norman. Does he treat you well? Are you happy with your lord?"

Beatrice had noticed the thin scar on her daughter's cheek and her heart quailed at the possibility that Edith had been bound to a man who took his pleasure in beating helpless women. Edith noticed the direction of her mother's gaze and her hand crept up to cover the cheek.

"My lord is most kind and considerate. He does not beat me, and his rages are few and soon over with. I am content, mother, with my life, and more than content with my lord. You have no need to worry over me, or indeed over Mathild and Edwina."

Beatrice's cheeks flushed a little guiltily. She had not thought to ask about her other daughters. She had been fully occupied with the presence of this, her favourite of the three girls she had birthed.

"Your sisters also fare well then? I had my doubts about Mathild and her attitude towards the Lord Ralf."

"Yes, I too was worried for a time, but Ralf is so good and has been very patient with Mathild. I am sure he has at least won her respect and affection."

At that moment Thrya and one of Lady Beatrice's serving girls knocked and entered with water and cloths for Edith to wash and two of Edith's men were shown in with her belongings. The next quarter of an hour flew by with exclamations over Edith's finery; the robes made up from the fine cloth which Michel had given her before her wedding, and of course her bride-gift; the beautiful necklace which Edith had not been able to resist bringing with her to show to her mother.

Lady Beatrice was speechless for a moment as the necklace twisted and turned in the light, almost dazzling in its beauty.

"Your lord must love you well to be so generous, Edith. You are a very lucky girl and I thank God that you have been so blessed."

Edith murmured some words of agreement, turning away from her mother and blinking away a silly rush of tears. If only her lord did love her as she loved him, she would count herself the most fortunate of women.

When the two ladies were ready, they descended to the hall for the evening meal. Edith sat at her father's left as befitted her new station in life, and as the conversation rose and fell, her eyes roved the hall watching her Norman escort now eating and drinking quite amicably with her father's Saxon men. Her mind insisted on recalling the last time they had sat here and she found it difficult to concentrate on her father's anxious enquiries about the Norman king and his attitude towards the Saxon lords who has sworn to him. At least she was able to reassure him that William's policy seemed now to be one of conciliation and the fact that his daughters were married or betrothed to favoured Norman lords guaranteed that Lord Rufus would be left in peace on his lands.

When the meal was finished Edith pleaded the long journey and her tiredness as an excuse to retire and after fondly embracing her mother and father Edith escaped thankfully to bed.

She lay sleepless for a while, wanting Michel with every fibre of her being, then the travelling took its toll and she drifted off into a light disturbed sleep, a sleep in which her lord fought with a Saer de Friese who had assumed gigantic proportions and who wielded a blade which was ten feet long.

After a restless night Edith yawned and stretched, rubbing the grit from her eyes as Thrya came in with the maidservant, carrying water to wash with and some warmed milk and bread to break her fast.

Edith shivered a little as she splashed the cold water onto her face and tried to banish the dreams which had left her feeling depressed and irritable. As her face emerged from the soft linen towel she raised her eyes to the blue sky visible through the window and taking a deep breath she blew out gustily and shrugging away her dreary thoughts turned briskly to don one of her older gowns and a pair of soft leather boots. She would not ride today, she would walk instead, following the old familiar paths of her former life here at Sensgarth, before the dark Norman lord had appeared to shake up her life and leave her bewildered with the passion he stirred within her.

A knock at the entrance to the room made her turn, and a swift smile lit up her face as her mother entered.

"Did you sleep well my dove, after your tiring journey?"

"Of course mother," lied Edith, "It is good to be home at Sensgarth and I intend to relax and be a positive sluggard for as long as I am able."

Lady Beatrice laughed indulgently as they left the room

together to descend to the hall. Edith's father stood by the fireplace in an attitude so reminiscent of the time when he had disclosed the terms of his daughters' marriages that Edith halted for a moment in her tracks, then she brushed her hand over her eyes and smiled a greeting.

Lord Rufus merely nodded and grunted a good morning to the two women, tugging thoughtfully at his long moustache as they moved to the chairs at the side of the fire. Edith was used to her father's taciturn manner, indeed he had spoken more to her since her arrival the previous day than he had since her childhood and she smiled wryly to herself at the difference her change of status had made to his attitude towards her.

For perhaps half an hour or so, Edith and her mother chatted amicably, but Edith's eyes kept straying to the bright sunshine streaming through the windows until finally her mother sighed and patted Edith's hands.

"I think a little fresh air would do you good my love. You need colour in your cheeks for you seemed a little pale this morning."

Trying not to seem over eager to leave her mother so soon, Edith was unable to prevent her eyes lighting up as she rose from her chair and her mother signed to a servant to fetch Gerd for his mistress's instructions.

"I must admit to a desire to feel the sun on my face and retrace my childhood haunts. After all it may be some time before I am able to visit you again."

Lady Beatrice's eyes dropped to her daughter's stomach and she queried gently, "Are you then with child, my Edith? For if you are then you must take things easy and not jeopardise the chances of an heir for your lord."

Edith blushed hotly at her mother's words then stammered a swift denial.

"No mother, there is no sign as yet..."

"Huh!" interrupted her father, "I hope you do your duty by your lord, with none of your headstrong ways and foolish fancies. If you are not breeding by now, the Norman should not have let you leave his side. You must be more careful that he does not put you aside as barren and find himself a more fertile wife.''

A stab of unreasoning terror struck at Edith's heart and she paled before the thought. Surely Michel would not find it so easy to repudiate her and replace her with another to bear his sons. She remembered his passion and his tenderness, then his rage when he had thought her in danger and she calmed somewhat. Surely his actions proved that he valued her as something more than a brood mare, although in that moment she decided to take all the measures available to her to ensure that she conceived as quickly as possible. She must not give him the slightest excuse to banish her from his side for that would surely break her heart. She was distracted by the arrival of Gerd as he entered the hall, bobbing apologetically to Lord Rufus and Lady Beatrice.

''You sent for me my lady?''

Edith smiled into the ugly familiar features of the Norman serjeant and banishing the worried thoughts from her mind she moved forward briskly, tossing a request for her short jacket to Thrya who hovered uncertainly in the background.

''I wish to walk out today Gerd, but I shall not need you to accompany me. There is no danger for a daughter of this house in the woods and fields hereabouts.''

''I beg pardon my lady, but my lord said I was not to leave your side for one moment. Indeed he would have my head from my shoulders if anything else were to happen to you whilst you were in my care,'' protested Gerd.

''Anything else?'' queried Lady Beatrice anxiously. ''Why Edith, what has befallen you to make your lord so wary of danger?''

''Nothing mother, 'tis nothing but a husband's tender care for a wife away from his side for the first time... All will be well Gerd. I know this land as well as I know my own palm and I wish to be alone for a while to relax and regain my spirits. I promise I shall take care and be back for my midday meal. Now stop worrying over me and take Thrya for a walk by the river. I am sure she could do with some diversion after the long journey."

As Gerd opened his mouth to continue his protests, he caught Thyra's eye over Edith's shoulder, and the maid gave a slight shake of her head with a warning frown. Gerd changed what he had been about to say and with a murmured, "As you wish my lady," moved to Thyra's side as she helped her mistress on with the doeskin hunting jacket which Edith had been used to wearing before her marriage. It had been rediscovered in the chests of clothing left behind when they had first left Stensgarth.

Edith smiled her thanks at Thyra and with a reassuring nod to Gerd Edith left the hall. Pausing at the top of the steps, she raised her face to the warm sun for a moment, then bending down she lifted the hem of her skirts to tuck them into her belt as the serf women did when gathering wood in the forests.

Pushing her hands into the folds of the jacket the Lady du Fourmeils left her father's hold, her eyes and her mind on the paths into the woods and on the song of the birds about her.

Thyra and Gerd and the Lady Beatrice watched her retreating back for several minutes until a bend in the path hid her from sight, then dipping a bow to the Lady of Stensgarth, Thrya slipped back into the hall to fetch her cloak and Gerd turned away to collect his weapons and don his leather hauberk. He met Thrya once more at the foot of the steps and without a word the couple turned to follow the path which their lady had taken.

Edith wandered for some time with her mind a complete blank, absorbing the sights and smells and sounds of the familiar surroundings, then finally she stopped in a small clearing and spying a fallen tree trunk she seated herself comfortably on the soft green moss with her back against the smooth bark of the fallen beech tree. Drawing up her knees she wrapped her arms about them and leaned her head back until it lay against the tree trunk, raising her soft brown eyes to the leafy canopy over her head.

For a while she let her thought drift, idly watching the

branches of the trees swaying and bobbing gently above her, then inevitably her mind turned to images of her husband.

Instead of fighting to dismiss all thoughts of him from her brain, she closed her eyes and dwelt on the flash of his even white teeth as he smiled and the strength of his lean fingers, the lift of corded muscle in his shoulders as he raised his sword in practice in the court at Tierand, the velvety whisper of his voice in her ear as he pressed close to her at night and the warmth of his mouth when he fastened demanding lips to hers.

Gritting her teeth and clenching her hands into fists Edith opened her eyes on the silent vow that should her lord survive the combat with de Friese, and she prayed God and all the saints that he would, she would use every means at her disposal to win his love and bind him to her so that he would be content at her side.

On this thought her breath caught at a stealthy rustle in the trees behind her. Scrambling to her feet, Edith whirled about in time to catch a glimpse of a fleeting shadow seeking concealment.

"Hold!" Her voice rang out clear and unafraid. Whoever it was, this was her father's land and although times had changed since the Normans had crossed to England, Lord Rufus' power was still strong enough to ensure his daughter's safety on his own holding.

"Come out and show yourself, whoever you are."

After a moment of silence two figures emerged from the trees and Edith stared incredulously at her maid and her serjeant who shuffled their feet and looked at each other sheepishly.

"Gerd! Thyra! I thought I made my wishes crystal clear..." Edith began heatedly, then at the crestfallen expressions on their faces Edith could not help but start laughing. "Oh, you are beyond hope. I told you that I would be perfectly safe here, yet still you insist on this over-protective attitude."

"Yes my lady, but it is always best to be safe, than sorry after," mumbled Gerd, red-faced but determined.

"And my lady, it will be time to eat if we start back now," added Thyra to distract Edith's attention from the burly serjeant and give him time to recover from his embarrassment.

"Very well then," sighed Edith resignedly although truth to tell her stomach was feeling a litle hollow and she turned almost eagerly back onto the path.

"I shall tell my lord on our return what faithful watchdogs he sent with me and no doubt he will wish to show his gratitude in some way," said the lady slyly, glancing beneath her lashes at the two walking to one side of her. She caught the bright glance which passed between them and bit her lip on a smile. Her suspicions were confirmed. There was more than mere companionship between the serjeant and her young maid, although Edith did not think that Thyra had taken Gerd to her bed as yet. However judging by the exchange of looks and the touching of hands, the temptation was very near the surface. Edith resolved to speak to Michel about it at the very first opportunity. She cut the thought before it was born that perhaps she would never see him alive again.

All the way back to the hold Edith kept the dark fears at bay and when she entered the bright bustle of the hall for her meal she smiled and chatted, denying the gnawing worm of despair within her.

As Lady Beatrice took her daughter around her herb garden picking out certain plants to be taken back to Tierand to make up the shortages in Edith's own small garden, Edith refused to consider the horror of life without her lord. It was only as she lay in bed that night, when all was dark and silent about her that the nightmares spread their fearsome wings and she stuffed the furs against her mouth to stifle her sobs until she came to the decision born of despair.

Her lord had decreed that she should remain at her father's hall until she heard the news of the outcome of the combat or until he should send for her, but she now determined to go against his wishes and rejoin her husband at Tierand. If he had left for William's court, well then she would follow him and she would not care if he should beat her so long as she could be at his side. She would at least know what was happening instead of falling prey to her worst fears and imaginings the moment she was alone. Her mind made up, and the action decided upon, the nightmares receded and the lady's eyes fluttered closed, her breathing soon even and steady as she slept.

It was the following morning when she arose with an eagerness she had forgotten she was capable of that she realised that she must surely disappoint her mother when she discovered Edith was leaving almost as soon as she had arrived. It would be easy to excuse herself to her father by saying that she realised how right he was when he said she should not have left her lord and was taking his advice and returning to the Norman at once. Her mother would not accept this however. She knew Edith better than Lord Rufus did. Perhaps Edith would have to be completely open with her mother and admit the truth.

As it was Edith was saved the trouble of any explanations or excuses.

After she had eaten Edith went down to the hall and was preparing to broach the subject of her departure when a commotion outside in the hold made her pause at the foot of the stairs. Lady Beatrice moved to her side as the door to the hall opened and Gerd ushered in a weary, dishevelled soldier whose eyes sought the Lady Edith, bowing his head before her as he handed her a roll of parchment tied up in doeskin.

"From my Lord du Fourmeils to the Lady Edith," he said respectfully.

Edith acknowledged him with a nod of her head and looked over his shoulder to Gerd hovering behind him.

"Gerd, a drink for my lord's messenger and some food."

"Yes my lady." Although Gerd was obviously deeply curious as to the contents of the letter, he did as he was told, and the messenger muttered his thanks as Gerd led him away.

When the door had closed behind her serjeant, Edith handed the parchment to her father to read. Although Lord

Rufus himself could read and write, he had never even considered teaching or having taught his wife and daughters. Edith watched anxiously therefore as her father swiftly scanned the letter until with a triumphant "Hah! The Norman has some sense after all." He raised his eyes to his daughter and grinned.

"Your lord has been summoned to William's court. Your presence also is required by the King so you are to join your husband in London as speedily as possible."

Edith's emotions ran the gamut from intense joy at the prospect of returning to Michel, to stomach churning fear at the realisation that her lord's contest with Saer de Friese was now a certainty. William would not have sent for them both if he did not intend to grant her lord's request for satisfaction on the tourney field.

Edith turned to her mother who was trying bravely to hide her disappointment at her daughter's imminent departure. Placing an arm about her shoulders Edith set about consoling her as they moved away to pack her belongings.

As the trunks were readied, Gerd appeared in the doorway in response to his lady's summons and was quickly informed of the situation.

"Yes my lady. I shall send two men to collect your chests." Gerd could not hide his delight at the change in plans and gave Thrya a surreptitious slap on the buttocks as he left the room. Edith raised her eyebrows at the byeplay but said nothing in the face of Thyra's obvious embarrassment.

Within the hour they were ready and as Edith embraced her mother and father in farewell, Lady Beatrice smiled bravely and joked, "My dove, you seem always to be coming and going without rest these days."

"Yes, 'tis true that I seem to be more upon my horse's back than at the loom or the embroidery frame," laughed Edith, unable to contain her high spirits.

"If the Norman has any sense, he'll tie you down with a swarm of brats," growled her father to cover his feelings.

Then Gerd lifted Edith to her palfrey's back and once again

the Lady du Fourmeils took to the road. This time to London to witness her lord's talents on the tourney field.

"And may God aid him." Edith prayed as she urged her horse onwards.

Michel had also made fast time on the road to London. The summons from the King had arrived only three days after Edith's departure, when the lady had gone too far to return. All her lord could do was send a fast messenger after her, bidding her meet him in London. He dare not wait for Edith to return to Tierand before setting off, as William's summons had included the words, 'with all speed.' The King would not wait, and Michel did not wish to prejudice his cause by arriving late.

He could only hope that de Friese did not learn that he and Edith were travelling separately and make another attempt to take his lady.

The black rage surged up within him as it always did at the thought of Edith in the power of his cousin. He must learn to control it as he would need every ounce of cold calculation and deadly calm when he faced Saer over their lances. His thoughts strayed back to Edith. The Norman lord was reluctant to admit to himself how much he missed his wife; and not merely in the bedchamber. He cursed himself for being so off-hand with her when she had left, but if he had weakened he would have forced her to stay at his side and she had seemed so eager to go, to get away from him so soon after he had brought her home. He knew that she welcomed his love-making. It was out of bed that their problems seemed to arise.

She closed her mind to him and spat defiance at every turn. It seemed he could do nothing right although he had never had any trouble handling women before this. Still, let him get the contest with de Friese over and he could then turn his full attention to capturing his wife's heart. The thought startled him briefly, then as he allowed his mind to accept it a smile curved his firm mouth. Was this then the love that the court ladies fluttered and sighed over? If it was it bore no relation to the ploys and scheming of those same ladies. Edith's actions bore no relation to them either, therefore he could admit his heart was hers. At least he could admit it to himself if not yet to his Saxon lady.

It was with fresh purpose and determination then that Michel finally reached London, seeking the same inn at which he and Lord Ralf had stayed previously and the landlord, remembering the Norman as a generous guest, bowed his delight at seeing him again.

"My lady wife will also be joining me within the next day or so. I want your very best chamber and make sure that it, and everything in it is clean and fresh."

"Yes lord. Of course lord. My humble roof is at your disposal."

Michel dismissed him with a coin and a wave of his hand then turned to wash, and change his clothes before making his presence known to William.

The King kept him waiting for a while before having him shown into the room. As Michel entered, William finished signing some papers, sanded them and handed them to his clerk before waving him away and regarding the dark-eyed lord with a frown. Then with a sigh he picked up Michel's letter from the small table at his side.

"My Lord du Fourmeils these are serious charges you lay to your cousin. Do you still hold by what you have written here?"

"Sire, the Lord de Friese has commited grievous crimes against me and mine. I do but ask for justice and the chance to prove my right on his body in lawful combat."

William caught his bottom lip between his fingers, then going off the subject for the moment he asked abruptly, "Your lady? Is she with you as I requested?"

Michel almost groaned at the question, then looking William straight in the face, he made the admission he had been hoping to avoid.

"Forgive me Sire. My lady wife had already left on a visit to her parents when your messenger arrived..."

"So soon after her terrible ordeal?" interrupted William somewhat sarcastically.

"She felt the need to get away from the scene of her abduction and relax in gentler surroundings for a while. I immediately sent after her and she is expected to join me in a day or so. I am sure she will be delighted to be presented to you."

"Yes. You have not said how you recoverd your wife my lord, but I expect the lady will be able to tell me the story herself when she arrives. In the meantime..." William gestured to a guard.

"Fetch me here the Lord de Friese."

They waited without speaking until there was a knock and the door opened to reveal the heavy figure of Saer de Friese.

Michel gave no sign of emotion as Saer bowed before William, ignoring Michel completely.

"Sire, you sent for me?"

At the sound of his strange high-pitched voice a frown flickered across William's face and his voice was cold as he answered, "My Lord de Friese, your cousin has made some serious accusations against you and has issued a challenge that you meet him body to body to prove his right. What say you to this?"

"I shall be more than happy to answer the challenge Sire. I dispute du Fourmeil's right to the lands he claims on the grounds that it was not his mother's right to inherit from her father. I have but attempted to set things right in the face of stubborn opposition and violence."

A sharp hissed intake of breath was the only sign that his

words had had any effect on Michel. His face was rigid as he
kept his fury under control and his dark eyes were like black
ice as he stared at his enemy.

William also kept his face expressionless as he delivered his
judgement.

"Very well. My lords you shall present yourselves on the
tourney field two days hence in readiness to prove your claims
one way or the other. And may God's will be done."

At his gesture of dismissal the two lords bowed before their
King and turned to leave the room but Michel halted as William
called his name.

"My Lord du Fourmeils?"

"Sire?"

"As soon as your lady arrives we shall expect to see you at
the court to dine. Be sure you do not forget." A slight inflexion
on the last word and Michel damned the King's eyes under his
breath as Saer's eyes widened and a cruel smile curved his lips
at the realisation that Edith was not with her lord but was still
on the road to London, presumably with a small escort. His expression changed however as the King added, "I shall send an
escort of my own men out on the road to the north to ensure
your lady's safe arrival," a pause then, "Thank you my lords."

Michel and Saer bowed once more then left, neither one
glancing now at the other. Once outside the room Michel
turned to descend the stairway but felt his arm taken in a
heavy grip. He turned and looked into the eyes of his enemy.

"Take your filthy paws off me you cur." he snarled, and Saer
let go his hold and raised his hands placatingly.

"Now now my lord, we do not want to cause a stir outside
the King's own chamber do we? I merely wish to assure myself
that your lady is well and that your estates are prospering. I
have no desire to saddle myself with a sickly woman and an
impoverished inheritance."

Michel was speechless with rage for several seconds then his
eyes narrowed as he realised the intent behind Saer's provok-
ing words. Coolly he allowed his stiff features to relax into a
sneer.

"I would not think that you would have a use for any woman, in good health or bad, my lord, and when I have finished with you, you will not be in any condition to worry over the state of my lands."

With that Michel turned on his heel and strode down the stairs to call for his horse and make his way back to the inn.

His thoughts were dark and disturbed as his horse clopped slowly back into the inn yard and Arnaud took one glance at his lord's face as he took the reins from him and deemed it wisest to say nothing.

Michel cast his cloak over a chair as Ranulf knelt to undo his master's sword belt, taking the weapon carefully away to clean and sharpen it. The squire had already spent the afternoon cleaning and burnishing the lord's mail; checking it meticulously for any defective links which may need mending, for the Norman's life could depend on his shirt of mail in the coming contest.

Sitting on the edge of the bed Michel dropped his head in his hands, rubbing his fingers over his face wearily as he thought back over his interview with the King.

It was always difficult to know what William was thinking but Michel decided that there had been certain indications that William favoured the cause of the Lord du Fourmeils. Why? He did not know. Possibly it was the way Saer had handled his attempt to take Michel's stronghold; possibly William had discovered Saer's disturbing preferences and this had disgusted him. He was known for his fidelity to his wife and his abhorrence of sexual perversion.

Oh God, when would Edith arrive? Please the saints it would be before the tourney. He needed her soft brown gaze and warm lips on his skin.

He groaned in despair, then his head jerked up at the sound of shouts and the clatter of horses' hooves in the yard of the inn. Surely Saer would not have been so lunatic as to attack him here. His heart stopped for the space of one beat as the sound of a lady's laugh floated up through the window. For a second he could not move, then he leapt for the door, taking the stairs two at a time until he burst out into the courtyard, and there she was! Laughing at a jest from Arnaud, her hair falling down from its braids as usual, the serjeants jostling to lift her down from her palfrey, moving back as Michel swallowed the constriction in his throat and moved forward to gaze up at her before raising his arms for her to slide down into his embrace.

Edith looked up into the beloved dark eyes as she stood within the circle of his arms, then her lord seemed to collect himself and turned with his hand on Edith's arm. His eyes swept the assembled company, silencing them with the haughtiness of his gaze, before catching sight of the innkeeper. He raised his voice. "Good 'keeper, a barrel of your best ale for my men to celebrate my lady's return."

A howl of delight went up from Michel's men but he caught Arnaud's arm and bent to murmur in his ear, "I still expect to sleep secure tonight, Arnaud. See to it."

"Fear not my lord. You will be as safe as the King himself."

Michel's lips twitched at the burly serjeant's avowal then he turned to escort Edith up to their room.

Thrya was following closely behind her mistress as they mounted the stairs but as they reached the door of the chamber, Michel stepped back and stretched his arm across to bar the maid's way.

"Thank you Thrya," he grinned, "You may go now and settle into your own quarters. I shall see to my lady's needs. We shall call you when we need you."

"Yes lord." Thrya flashed a knowing smile at the Norman, then turned away with a swish of her skirts to descend eagerly to join Gerd.

Edith was standing facing him as he moved into the room and closed the door firmly behind him. He said nothing, merely crossed to a small table by the bed, on which stood a flagon of wine. Pouring a cupful with unsteady hands he turned to offer it to his wife and to take her cloak from her shoulders, controlling the urge to take her in his arms and crush her to him.

"And now my lady, explain if you will how you came here so quickly. You were gone three days before my messenger was sent after you."

"We left immediately he arrived, lord, and we did not spare our horses as I thought there was some urgency for us to arrive here."

He stared at her as she spoke, his eyes taking in the dust on her clothes, the lines of weariness around her mouth and eyes, eyes which nevertheless sparkled with some inner agitation as she waited for him to reply.

"Do you feel able to dine at the court tonight? William is eager to meet you and has commanded our presence as soon as you arrive."

"Whatever is your desire my lord. If it will further our cause to dine with William tonight then by all means let us do so."

At that moment Michel wanted to shout at her that his desire was not to dine with William. His desire was to take his wife in his arms after what seemed centuries without her, and make passionate love to her until she cried for mercy. However, he could not do that. Not yet. He must get this damned fight out of the way first, then he could take his lady home and prove to her his love and desire.

"Did all go well with the King my lord?" asked Edith anxiously, and Michel swung away from her moodily.

"The tourney takes place in two days' time."

That was all. The abrupt statement made Edith pale, then she smiled determinedly and set down her cup of wine.

"Well my lord, if we are to dine with the King this evening I had best make myself presentable. I would not wish to cause you shame before the court." She moved swiftly to the door before he could prevent her, and shouted for Thrya.

As the maid entered, Michel pushed past, muttering about seeing to hot water for his lady's bath and clattered down the stairs with face black as a thundercloud.

Thrya glanced at her mistress but Edith merely turned away with a smile and the women spent the afternoon unpacking. Edith sank gratefully into the tub of hot water when it arrived, hauled puffingly up the stairs by two servants.

Michel returned to the chamber to prepare for the visit to court, but he seemed silent and withdrawn so Edith kept her peace, being content for the moment just to be with him.

She was cool and calm when presented to William and the King seemed impressed with her modesty and the intelligent but reserved way in which she replied to all his questions.

There was no sign of Saer at the court that night so Michel forced himself to relax and forget, so far as he was able, the forthcoming combat.

As Michel and Edith took their leave, the King's face was serious as he bid them farewell for the moment.

"Believe me, my Lord du Fourmeils, when I wish you well in the tourney and my Lady Edith, should you ever require my protection or my aid you have only to ask. I thank you for your gracious presence this evening. Goodnight."

Michel and Edith bowed low before him, then made their way slowly back towards the inn. Michel's hands were solicitous as he lifted Edith down from her palfrey and in spite of her weariness Edith's pulses leapt at his touch.

Dismissing Thyra, almost as soon as they were alone Edith found herself swept into impatient arms with hungry, demanding lips on hers. She thought he would crush the very breath from her body as he strained her to him and she fought for release, gasping as he let her go to turn away, running his hand agitatedly over his hair.

"Forgive me my lady. I realise how tired you must be after your arduous journey and the strain of the court this evening. If you wish I shall lie elsewhere in order that you may sleep in peace."

Edith's eyes were tender and her voice full of love as she answered.

"My lord, had I travelled a thousand leagues more and attended one hundred such banquets as tonight, I would still wish to lie at your side."

He stared at her incredulously for several seconds, then as her eyes shyly fell before his, he moved forward and swept her into his arms. She closed her eyes and gave herself up to the fierce longing which had tormented her mind and body through all the days without him and Michel drank his fill from the heavy draught of love that night.

When Edith awoke the following morning, Michel had already left her side, but as Thyra fussed over her with her breakfast, the door flew back on its hinges and he whirled into the room.

"Come, you lazy wench, 'tis time you were up and about. I do not intend to sit and brood for the next two days. We shall enjoy our trip to the city."

Throwing open Edith's chest he hauled out some of her clothes, picking out a moss green gunna and leaf-coloured bliaut to toss on the bed.

"Come my lady, make haste. I shall wait for you below."

Edith crammed the food hastily down her and dressed at record speed, flying down the stairs to the yard where her husband waited with the horses ready saddled.

"My lord?" she hesitated and Michel's brows drew together.
"Yes, what is it?"

"My lord, do you not think we could dispense with the horses for a while. Truly I feel as though I have four legs instead of two, I have spent so much time on horseback."

With a shout of laughter echoed by the men around them Michel slid down to the ground and offered Edith his arm.

"Lady Edith I am yours to command. If you wish to walk, then walk we shall."

That day passed in a whirl as did the next, visiting the fairs and stalls in and around London. Her lord seemed determined to enjoy the two days before he staked all on his ability to wield his sword and aim his lance more skilfully than his opponent.

The night before the tourney his lovemaking was wild and urgent. His hands bruised her flesh and his teeth left marks which she touched the next day with tender fingers. At the height of his passion he had crushed her to him as though he would fuse her body with his and she thought he whispered "my love," sending her joy beyond bounds.

When they awoke next morning, however, he was silent and withdrawn. William had decreed that the Lady Edith sit with him on the day of the tourney..."to ensure the lady's safety and well-being."

In a way Edith was glad because, although it meant she could not arm her lord as she would have wished, she was forced to display a calm and even mien in front of the court and in front of Saer at whom she might otherwise have screamed her rage and hate.

Edith wore a russet gunna and a plain bliaut, and around her neck blazed Michel's bride gift, a luminous magnet for the eyes of the court ladies. William too bent his glance to the magnificent necklace and complimented Edith on her husband's generosity.

"Were my lord's gift to me nothing but child's beads I would wear them this day in his honour Sire," stated Edith proudly, making clear to all her feelings for her lord. William smiled stiffly and inclined his head to acknowledge her brave words then turned his attention to the combatants.

The air was heavy and still as the heralds called the throngs of lords and ladies to witness the dispute between Michel du Fourmeils, Lord of Tierand and Quatre Bras and Saer de Friese of Charbonnay: that each should attempt to prove his claim to certain lands and titles on the body of the other. And may God aid the arms of the right.

The two lords rode slowly from the ends of the lists to dip their lances before William. Saer made an impressive figure as he straddled his great roan destrier making Edith's lord look light and slim on his young chestnut horse. The danger, indeed, lay in the inexperience of Michel's young warhorse, unproven as yet in the strain of battle.

Michel's eyes slid from William, to Edith sitting at the King's side and on a sudden impulse Edith stood and unclasping the tawny girdle from her waist, held it out to her lord. Her eyes met his and she tilted her chin proudly and smiled, then a murmur of approval rustled through the court ladies as Michel lowered his lance, and hooking her favour on the tip, it slid to his hand. He raised it to his lips to kiss before tying it around his upper arm and pulling it tight with his teeth, his eyes never leaving hers as he did so.

A sneer crossed the face of the watching Saer de Friese and he leaned to murmur, "How like you your lady's pretty face now my lord?"

Michel went white and in a low menacing tone replied.

"You, you foul cur will not come out of this with your head still on your shoulders. I shall remove it from your diseased and corrupt body, and rid the earth of an unbearable stench, thus doing all mankind a favour."

Saer's face turned purple with rage, and a half supressed titter ran through the court. William controlled his features with difficulty. De Friese should have known better than to taunt du Fourmeils about his wife, when it was obvious that the lord was besotted with the Saxon lady.

He signalled to the two combatants to take their places and they turned their horses' heads and cantered to opposite ends of the lists, black rage clouding Michel's vision and making his hands tremble.

Ranulf was waiting for his lord with a lance ready and Michel took a deep controlling breath and determinedly ordered his shaking limbs. He must not fail, too much was at stake. He touched Edith's girdle where he had tied it round his arm, and a dangerous smile hovered round his lips. He would be worthy of his Saxon falcon this day or die in the attempt.

The marshal called the knights to order and Michel saw Saer

lower his lance. He aimed his own lance to Saer's breast and urged his young horse forward at the marshal's signal.

The two lords thundered down the lists towards each other, Michel slanting his shield across his body as he realised that Saer's lance tip was aimed straight at his chest. Because Saer was so much larger and heavier than Michel, it meant that Edith's lord must avoid a direct clash with the other knight and attempt to deflect Saer's lance away from his body with his shield.

The impact was terrific as Michel's lance caught Saer full on his shield at the same time throwing his own body to the side and pushing his shield up and away, sending Saer's weapon skidding over Michel's shoulder and into the air. The combination of the force of Michel's blow on his shield and the effect of his own lance meeting no solid target sent Saer de Friese crashing out of his saddle and onto the ground.

There was a roar of approval from the spectators. Only Edith sat silent, her eyes closed, her fists clenched tight. Then she forced her lids open and she felt a surge of relief as she realised that the man on the ground was Saer and her lord was at that moment hauling his mount to a halt, throwing down his lance to draw out his heavy sword.

Saer pushed himself to his feet, struggling to regain the breath which had been knocked out of him by the fall, and also unsheathing his sword. The two men circled each other warily, watching for an opening, then with a high-pitched shriek, Saer swung his sword at Michel's head. Michel ducked under the blow, then raised his own sword to thrust at Saer's unprotected side. With a mighty effort Saer reversed the direction of his sword and there was a terrific clash as the two weapons caught and slid off each other. Then it was Michel's turn to take the initiative: He lunged forward with the point of his sword straight at Saer's eyes and Saer was forced to throw himself to one side to avoid the deadly point of the weapon. As he hit the ground he threw his legs up, tripping Michel as he stepped forward, and swinging his sword around to bite into the upper muscles of Michel's arm.

Edith uttered no sound as the blood spurted and her lord went down. Her eyes were fixed on the scene with glittering intensity – her face as white as chalk, a drop of blood showing where she had bitten through her bottom lip.

Saer surged to his feet and raised his sword to slay his fallen opponent but with a superhuman effort Michel forced himself to his knees and with a mighty thrust sent the point of his weapon slicing through mail and flesh into Saer's chest. Broken links caught on the edge of the sword – A testimony to a squire's carelessness –. Saer stood transfixed, his sword still raised above his head, then the blood gushed from his mouth and he toppled forward to lie jerking in the dirt at Michel's feet.

There was silence as the dust settled and Michel pushed himself upright to stand swaying above the body of Saer de Friese, then he bent to pick up Saer's sword and turned to William. William gave an impassive nod and Michel swung the sword into the air bringing down with all his force to sever his enemy's head from his body. The whole court came to its feet and as Edith struggled to push her way through to her lord, he crumpled in a heap next to the headless corpse.

Ranulf and Gerd reached Michel only seconds before Edith, and Gerd examined his master's wound grimly before gently lifting him with Ranulf and carrying him carefully to their own end of the lists. A litter was quickly constructed and Lord Michel was laid upon it to be carried back to their room at the inn.

As Edith organised the removal of her lord, a knight stood at her side and bowed respectfully. "King William's compliments my lady. If you have need for aught for your lord's or your own comfort you have but to ask. Confirmation of your lord's titles will be attended to without delay. May I add my own congratulations and sympathy at the same time. Your lord was magnificent and if you need any help I shall be only too glad to be of assistance." The knight's pretty speech reached Edith through a haze. She thanked him, scarcely knowing what she was doing, then moved away at the side of the litter bearing her wounded lord.

Once back at the inn she quickly gave orders for hot water and clean cloths, directing Ranulf to remove his master's mail as carefully as he could. In spite of the squire's care however, the wound started bleeding sluggishly again and Edith struggled to staunch the flow. Her heart contracted at the sight of Michel's drawn features but she cleansed his wound, and frowned at the torn muscle and flesh. She ordered Thyra to bring her a needle and thread. Expertly and neatly she sewed up her husband as she would stitch a gown, then applied clean pads to his arm binding it tightly. As she finished her ministrations Michel's eyes fluttered open and a pain-filled dark gaze sought hers. She fought to smile at him and his eyes softened as they rested on her anxious face.

"Full and terrible revenge my sweet falcon," he forced out hoarsely and she placed her finger on his lips to quiet him.

"Yea, lord, you took more than your due and my heart flies high that you should consider me worth such a price."

"That and more, lady," he got out, making Edith bite back the tears at his words before his lids closed once more and his breathing steadied to an even rhythm.

Edith watched over him throughout the night as he tossed and turned, muttering restlessly as she bathed his fevered body with cool cloths. At one point he suddenly started up wild-eyed and gasping, calling, "She is gone. She is gone. The falcon is flown."

Then as Edith threw her arms about him to restrain him, he laid his head to her breast and whispered, "Ah now, my love, my heart burns for you. Do not leave me."

Edith pushed him back onto the pillows, wiping the sweat from his skin and pressing her lips to the high cheekbones, murmuring reassurance as she would to a child. When he had quieted and was sleeping peacefully, Edith stretched herself carefully beside him with a sigh, hugging his words to herself as a charm.

For almost a week Edith cared unceasingly for her warrior, until the morning she awoke to find him leaning up on his elbow, watching her with tender eyes as she struggled to rise.

She smiled dazzingly at him, her heart full of joy to see his eyes clear and free from pain. Slowly he lowered his head and his lips traced the white line of the scar on her face, whispering her name with an aching fervance which made her heart hammer in her breast.

"My sweet Edith," Michel took a steadying breath, "Tell me now my sweet Saxon falcon, does this Norman lord hold your heart, or does it still fly free with no chains to bind it?"

Her eyes searched his for a moment, seeing the tension appear as she hesitated, then with a feeling as though she were plunging from a high cliff, the lady gave her answer.

"My lord, you are my life's joy. Without you I am as nothing; my eyes do not see the sky, my lips cannot taste the wine. My heart as well as my body belong to you and they will never change as long as I have life in my limbs."

For a moment her heart failed her as he made no reply, then her world spun about her as he made his avowal of love.

"Lady, from the moment I laid my eyes upon you, I knew that I had to have you for my own. My body cries out for you as now does my heart. If you should ever leave me or be taken from me then I would be as a raging lion without its mate, a madman forever condemned to hell on earth. Saxon falcon, you have my heart, my mind and my body in your keeping and I pray that you will never let them go."

With a sob Edith laid her scarred cheek to her husband's breast, and with all her doubts banished from her mind forever, gave herself up to the strong arms and insistent lips of her Norman lord. The Saxon falcon was home to roost.